J. M. Robson has been writing novels for a number of years and *I am the Walker* is her second novel to be published.

A lover of horror, thriller and mystery books, she spends her spare time reading, writing and researching ideas and locations for her next novels. She has recently completed the sequel to her first published horror novel, *Three Little Words*.

J.M. Robson lives with her husband and three rescue dogs in a small village on the outskirts of Dundee, Scotland. She has one son and two beautiful grandchildren. She supports a number of animal charities in the UK and abroad including "Help Bulgaria's Street Dogs and Cats" and a number of organisations in Romania.

I Am The Walker

Also by J.M. Robson

Three Little Words

J.M. Robson

I Am The Walker

Pegasus

A CIP catalogue record for this title is
available from the British Library

ISBN 978 1 910903 12 4

Pegasus is an imprint of
Pegasus Elliot MacKenzie Publishers Ltd.
www.pegasuspublishers.com

First Published in 2018

Pegasus
Sheraton House Castle Park
Cambridge CB3 0AX England

Printed & Bound in Great Britain

Dedication

A big thank you to Gail Souter, Margaret Souter, Ferdinand Vasquez, Gavin Forbes, Ryan Robson and Kelsey Moncrieff

For all the animal rescuers around the world including: Vinia, Janet, Gail, Scarlat, Uana, Marilena, Daniela, Roxana, Iri, Gera, Christa and Dani.

CHAPTER ONE

TIME TO TELL THE TRUTH

My name is Billy Donaldson and I'm going to tell you a story.

I live in Fort William, Scotland. I am twenty years old and I still live with my mother and father, Danny and Hilary Donaldson.

We live in a small, two-bedroom council house, in the working-class area of town. The grey exterior of the house could do with being painted and the inside is in dire need of decoration and modernisation.

I am not what you would call stunningly handsome, in fact to be brutally honest I am one of those men that most women wouldn't look at twice.

I have short, black, curly hair that gets really greasy if I don't wash it at least three times a week. I have green eyes, high cheekbones, thin lips and a button nose.

I am meant to wear glasses when I read, but I never do. I am always a bit spotty and should really take more care of my skin. As for having street cred or an image, well I don't have one. I like simple clothes: combat trousers, checked shirts and sensible shoes.

I am slender built, not muscular at all and average height. I look a lot younger than twenty and wouldn't get served in a bar without providing ID. Not that I have ever frequented a bar. I don't drink. My abusive, alcoholic father has put me off touching the stuff.

I am soft spoken, very polite, meek, modest and painfully shy. I would help anyone in need, even if I didn't know them which is probably one of my biggest faults. Basically, to the people I know, I'm a gullible fool. I let people use and abuse me and, even though I know I am being taken for a simpleton, I still can't stop myself from being so stupid.

My dad teases me about my sensitive nature. He calls me horrible names and makes fun of me in front of my mother, who does nothing to stop it.

Often, he reminds me of how much of a failure I am. He often tells me that he was sure that my mother was given the wrong child at the hospital where I was born. He is sure somewhere in the UK, his tall, strapping, handsome son lives with my real parents who are proud of his every accomplishment.

I have lived in Fort William all my life and work for my father's best friend, Mr McGregor. I have worked for him since the day I left school at the age of sixteen.

Mr McGregor owns a fishmongers and I work in the rear of the shop with his only son William, who is the same age as me. We spend all day washing and gutting fish. As you can imagine, it is a smelly, horrible job.

I love cheese on toast, hate bananas and am allergic to oranges. If I eat one, I come out in a rash that spreads from my face right down to my navel. It looks pretty nasty, so I don't eat them any more. I don't need to be doing anything that makes me look any worse than I already do.

I am not a big fan of television. I personally think it rots the brain. If more people took the time to read a book, visit a museum, or families spent quality time together then there would not be so many young delinquents wandering the streets causing bother.

I read a lot. I spend most of my evening and the weekends curled up on my bed with a good book. I love thrillers and crime stories. Especially ones based on historical events and older times.

I love rock music because you can play it loud and shout instead of sing. I sound like a wailing banshee when I try to sing so this kind of music suits me fine.

So basically, these are the most interesting facts about me and about my life. Nothing exciting, nothing unusual, nothing to make you want to become my friend. In fact, up until two months ago, I was practically invisible. My life had no bearing or consequence to anyone else, even my own parents. I existed and that was about it.

Then, in a blink of an eye, my life changed. Events forced my hand and after years of abuse, neglect and rejected love something inside me snapped.

This is the story of what happened. This is the story of my rebirth. The story of how a shadow, an individual that had lived their life up until now on the side-lines, became the centre of attention. The one that everyone would remember.

This is how I became a Scottish legend and a psychopathic killer.

So, let's start at the beginning.

CHAPTER TWO

THE BEGINNING OF THE END

I don't think there has been a day that has gone by when my father has not put me down or attacked me in some way with his evil, vicious tongue. All my dad ever wanted was a son: a strong, strapping, handsome lad that he could take hunting and drinking. A son that would like the same things as him. Someone that is the total opposite of me.

I once asked my mum why they never had any more children, especially seeing that I was a complete disappointment. She told me that after I was born that she had some woman problems and she had to have a hysterectomy. That put an end to any more offspring and it meant they were stuck with me.

That meant my father despised me even more. Not that I ever care that much about what he thinks but at times his sadistic, evil words can be really cutting. I remember the time I was sitting in the lounge with him and my mum.

It was a Sunday evening. We had just finished the traditional Sunday dinner that my mum had spent hours making and which my dad had devoured in minutes like a starving, uncivilised caveman.

The TV was on, as usual, and my father had just opened another can of beer, making it number eight for the evening.

"So, you little fuck up, when are you going to find some friends and start acting like a real human being," he asked before burping loudly.

I remember looking over at my mum. She didn't take her eyes from the TV, didn't say a word. Didn't stop the barrage of abuse.

"Do you know what people say about you?" he continued as he scratched his crotch.

It was disgusting to watch.

My dad had once been a handsome man but when I was born and he realised that I was going to be the only child he bore, he kind of just let himself go.

He drinks every day and to an excess that really isn't sustainable and eating habits, well healthy food is like poison to him. I am amazed he is still alive.

I didn't say anything. There was no point and if I did reply he would probably slap me. Even though he was asking me a question, my requirement was only to listen to his abuse.

"They say you are soft in the head. That something is wrong with you." He pointed a finger to the side of his head and then tapped it hard a few times.

He took a big slug of beer before continuing with his cutting, cruel words.

"Do you know what? I agree with them. You are a weirdo, my weirdo. I am stuck with you. Do you imagine how embarrassed it makes me and your poor mother?"

I turned to look at my mum as my dad continued his abuse.

She didn't respond or even act like she was interested in the conversation. She was blanking what was going on, just as she always did. It was as if she was sitting in a totally different room and couldn't see or hear what was happening.

I decided it was time to leave and go to my room. As I got to my feet my dad roughly grabbed my left wrist.

"Why can't you be like William? Why didn't I get a real son?" His red, rough and round face was contorted with anger.

He squeezed my wrist for a few seconds, hurting me. Then he finally let me go and I quickly made my getaway to my bedroom.

He is nothing more than a cruel, vicious-tongued, drunken bully. I hate him and despise spending any time with him, so as I get older and wiser, I try to spend less and less time at home.

I found this difficult at first. I don't like alcohol, I can't dance so discos and nightclubs were not an option and did I mention that I have no friends?

I'm a loner, always have been and always will be I suppose.

I can't see me ever finding that special someone when I don't participate in any activities that involve spending time with the opposite sex. The only time I speak to females is when I am at work and most of the customers I see are old, wrinkly women, who smell of mothballs and buy fish that can be poached and mashed down so it's easy to eat without their false teeth.

As you can imagine, sex is non-existent and I think I am the oldest virgin in town. The only relief I get is through self-gratification, an activity I'm not very proud of but everyone needs a bit of pleasure in their life.

I don't own any dirty magazines and never watch any porno movies. In fact, the thought of seeing a woman naked slightly unnerves me. I can't even look through the lady's underwear section of my mother's shopping catalogue without blushing, but hopefully one day I will meet someone that makes me feel special and will help me get over my intimacy fears.

As I said before I tried to find a hobby, something I could enjoy – alone. Then by chance I found something that I really would like to do.

I was watching television with my mum. Dad had gone to the pub and I think *Coronation Street* was on. I wasn't really watching the show, just pretending to.

My mum likes the company at night when Dad is in the pub. Goodness knows why she misses him when he goes out, but this isn't the time to discuss her.

Anyway, there was an advert about visiting Scotland. It showed the Highlands in all their glory: the stunning snow-capped peaks of Glencoe, the craggy rock faces of Ben Nevis and the lush green hills of Glencoe. Lochs and castles, eagles and kestrels, quaint villages and picturesque countryside flashed across the television screen while traditional bagpipe music played *Flower of Scotland.*

For the first time in my pathetic life I felt as if I belonged somewhere and it was right here on my doorstep. I could actually picture myself standing at the top of Ben Nevis or some other mountain, the toes of my boots protruding over the edge as I looked down at the small, faraway world below. I just knew that I could be whoever I wanted to be out there in the wilderness with only the grass, rocks, Scottish wildlife, sun and sky to keep me company.

The next day I spent three hundred and fifty pounds of my savings at the local outdoor adventure shop. It was like a thrill, an extreme buzz, something like what a junkie must feel when they are desperate for a fix and finally get to stick that dirty needle in their arm, releasing the drug that will fill them with oozy happiness and send them to that special place. I was finally going to do something that I really wanted to do. I was sure I skipped up the road with the shopping bags. I was so excited that the minute I got home I immediately tried on the clothes I had bought and admired myself in the mirror. For the first time ever, I think I looked quite dashing. The outdoor look actually suited me and I still think it does.

For the next two nights, I would go home from work and sit at my PC and look for possible walking routes. I know it's hard to believe that for someone who lives in the beautiful Highlands of Scotland that I didn't really know the first thing about my local surroundings. I guess that has a lot to do with my lack of interest in anything for a very long time. I would put it down to depression and the fact that I would spend most evenings at home with my parents, watching stupid soaps and crappy reality telly programmes that would numb the most active, brilliant mind.

By Saturday morning I was ready to head out on my first ramble. I decided on a gentle walk, nothing too strenuous, so I opted for a walk to the Inchree Falls. People had rated the walk on Trip Advisor and it got lots and lots of five-star reviews. Reviewers were saying it was a nice gentle walk with a gentle climb to the waterfall. Perfect for a newbie like me.

At eight a.m. that morning I donned my hiking boots, red checked shirt, black Gor-Tex trousers and gaiters before packing my rucksack.

That morning just like every morning I go walking, I pack my bag with enough food and water for three days. Even though I only intend to spend the one night away from home, I always make sure I will have enough supplies in case something goes wrong. I also pack my one-man tent, sleeping bag, blow-up pillow, waterproofs, first aid kit, rubbish bags, a toilet roll, matches, lighter, torch and digital camera. I also carry a small pot which doubles up as a kettle for my bedtime cocoa. Sometimes I take a wind-up radio, if I think I might feel like having a singsong at the campfire.

In my shirt pocket I have a compass, a small flick knife that I hadn't used very often and my map hangs around my neck in a waterproof pouch. I don't take any other home comforts, not even a book. I like to keep my mind clear of any distractions. The time on the mountains and hills is my time; it belongs to me.

But that first walk wasn't up to what I expected it to be. I thought I would walk about six hours, find a secluded spot, pitch my tent and settle down for an evening of peace and quiet. As soon as I got out of the car I knew that I had selected the wrong location.

The Glenrigh Forest car park was mobbed. Elderly couples, families and hiking parties were all there, getting ready for a walk through the forest to the falls. They were going the same way I was; there was going to be no seclusion. So much for my campfire and night under the stars alone. If I stayed here I would be surrounded by old people, married couples, giggling teenagers and moaning little brats. I suppose you can tell I don't interact well with many people.

Just as I didn't think I could feel any more depressed, the heavens above me opened and heavy rain poured from the sky, soaking my shirt right through to my skin before I had a chance to get my waterproof jacket out of my rucksack.

I felt so angry. I would say it was the first time in my life that I had felt a strong emotion. Every other feeling I had ever had before that moment were just wishy-washy, half-hearted feelings. I was really mad and actually felt like hitting someone – anyone. If one of the people in the car park had been stupid enough to approach me I don't think I would have been able to control my temper.

It was a really strange sensation to feel so worked up inside and I actually felt a little scared. To feel as if I could hurt someone was something I never ever expected and I had to get back in the car and give myself a moment or two to settle down and regain composure.

Once I had chilled, I decided it would be best to go on the walk anyway because I knew it would look strange if I got back in the car and drove away. So, I decided on a leisurely couple of hours stroll through the lush, green forest, selecting the route to get a view of the waterfalls.

The scenery was breathtaking and the smell, just amazing. After the heavy rain, you could smell the grass and the earthiness of the tree bark. I walked through the deciduous woodland that included hazel, rowan, oak and birch trees. Luscious green fern grew everywhere. I heard that red squirrels lived in the woods, but I wasn't lucky enough to see any. They were probably hiding in dry spots after the heavy rain and, as I walked through the forest, drops of water dripped from the trees and onto my waterproof jacket and trousers. My shirt was still wet underneath my jacket, but I didn't care or notice any more. I was mesmerised by my surroundings. It was stunningly beautiful.

As the walk climbed a little, I got a great view of Loch Linnhe. Even on a drab and wet day, the loch looked spectacular and I decided I needed to consider visiting the loch on one of my next rambles.

The next highlight of the walk was reaching the viewing point on the Abhainn Righ where the series of eight waterfalls cascade down the hillside; you don't get a full clear view, but it is still a sight to see.

I continued up the path, through the shrubby round and trees. As I got higher up, I met more and more people. This really was a popular destination.

Finally, I reached my destination, the second viewing point and from this higher angle I could clearly see all the waterfalls and the loch.

I loved the sound of the waterfalls. I so wished I could strip off and dive in, but it was a bit cold for it today. I watched as the waters flowed down between the lush, green and golden mountainside. I really wished I was a good artist. I would love to sit here and sketch the scenery, but my artwork extends to stick figures and trees so I would just have to take lots of pictures instead.

I must have taken about fifty pictures which was quite a feat as the place was buzzing and getting busier by the minute. A grey-haired pair of pensioners asked me if I could take their picture. I really didn't want to but did it anyway so I could get some peace and quiet to take the pictures I wanted.

I really needed to capture the moment. This was my first trip and I realised just how much I felt at one with nature and the Scottish Highlands. I loved it out here, in the open – no parents, no bullying cousin and I craved more of this. However, next time I needed it to be in a more secluded location, off the beaten track.

After a snack of a banana, energy bar and a bottle of apple juice, I headed back down to the car park.

I knew where I had to go and I got into my five-year-old, grey Volkswagen Polo and headed for the Glencoe visitor centre. I knew I would be able to pick up some leaflets there that would give me a better idea of where I could find the seclusion that I desperately needed.

I remember being taken to the visitor centre when I was fourteen years old. It was on a school trip. We were to visit the interaction area of the centre where you can see what it feels like to climb ice, learn about how Glencoe was formed and find out ways we could help save the environment.

I hated the trip. Being the shy, quiet, awkward type meant I stood out like a sore thumb. The staff took pity on me and mothered me the entire day. That meant the minute I got back on the school bus that I was subjected to a vicious attack from the class bully. He forced me to sit beside him and he hit me and slapped me while he called me a pussy and spat in my face.

So, I planned to slip in, get the information I wanted and leave before any of the over eager, helpful staff

24

noticed me and offered their assistance while they looked at me with their pitying eyes as they felt sorry for the geeky loner.

Getting in unnoticed was easy. The centre was busy with out-of-town tourists. A loud, middle-aged American couple dressed in shorts, T-shirts and bright, white trainers were hogging the attention of the one and only female attendant who was on duty that morning. Had they even noticed the weather outside? Did they realise how wet it was? I hoped they didn't plan hiking. They were so unprepared.

The female attendant was a short, overweight, red-headed woman with a freckly face and the most wonderful and beautiful smile. She looked as if she were about the same age as me. She was giggling and chatting with the couple as she helped them pick postcards and a selection of handmade sweeties that the gift shop sold.

She wore her long hair in a ponytail and was dressed in light blue jeans, white trainers and a green T-shirt with a picture of Glencoe printed on the front. The T-shirt was a bit too tight for her more than ample breasts and it pulled in the middle, making you notice her breasts even more. Not that I was staring at them like a pervert; her boobs just happened to catch my eye and I blushed the second I realised I was checking out a woman.

I liked the way she laughed. Her nose crinkled and her green eyes twinkled with fun and enjoyment.

I knew I had to stop looking at her. I was starting to feel like a peeping Tom.

I headed straight for the leaflets that were arranged on a stand next to the café entrance where they sell cakes, pastries, ice cream and tea. I had just selected a leaflet with a picture of Ben Nevis on the front, when I felt a warm hand on my still damp shoulder.

I just about jumped right out of my wet shirt. It had been the red-headed attendant. She laughed at how I had reacted and my face instantly turned red. She instantly apologised.

"Hi there, I am Sarah. Sarah Granger. I am one of the visitor centre assistants."

She extended her hand and even though I was nervous as hell, I placed my hand in hers and shook her hand.

She was so pretty, with emerald green eyes and a smattering of freckles across her button nose. I didn't realise I was shaking her hand a bit too long as I listened to her sweet voice as she spoke about the centre and the best places to ramble and climb in the area.

After I somehow managed to calm myself down and control the sex urges that were stirring in my pants, I told her my name and asked her for some advice on where to find a walking route that was quieter than the conventional tourist routes: something off the beaten track.

God, I was so smitten.

Her smile widened at my request.

"I am always happy to give advice to fellow lovers of the great outdoors. Especially one that is a local. Not enough people from around here take the time to get to know our beautiful countryside. Wait here for one moment. I have the perfect location for you."

She made her way around to the back of the desk where some more leaflets were displayed in a clear, Perspex frame.

It was a leaflet about Ben Nevis and the surrounding mountain groups, but it was a lot thicker and the map it included was very detailed. It showed routes to the top of the different mountains in the range that weren't often used by the everyday rambler. They were certainly more challenging and only experienced walkers and climbers frequented the routes.

"If you want to get off the usual tourist track, these walks are ideal for you," she said as she opened the map. "But you need to know some of them are quite challenging, so make sure you prep well before setting off."

I watched her as she outlined a couple of routes with her finger, telling me about the best viewpoints and if camping was permitted. She was so pleasant, so attentive. I was smitten but not brave enough to ask for her phone number.

"This one here is my favourite." She traced the route that led up Carn Mor Dearg. I wasn't familiar with the mountain, but if she liked it, I knew I would too.

I didn't tell Sarah that I was very inexperienced; for some reason she thought I had probably been up Ben Nevis more times than I could remember. So, I pretended that she was right and took the leaflet. I thanked her for her help before I left the tourist centre.

I walked back to the car with a big, stupid-looking grin on my face. I had never felt so good in all my life. A girl had actually spoken to me. She wanted to speak to me and seemed to be genuinely interested in me. Maybe in a couple of weeks' time I would return to the centre and ask her to accompany me on a walk.

Giddy with excitement and with the information from Sarah, I went home. I was so excited about the prospect of planning my next trip.

As I turned into the street where I live, I saw an ambulance parked in the driveway of our small, mid-terraced house.

My heart sank as I thought that maybe, finally, my father had totally lost the plot and after one drink too many had finally murdered my mother.

I was so distraught that I nearly crashed into another car coming in the opposite direction as I just couldn't take my eyes off the big white vehicle, with the blue flashing lights that signalled to me that something awful was waiting for me inside my home.

I brought the car to a sudden halt outside the house, the brakes squealed loudly and before I had even turned off the engine I was out of the car door and running up the pathway to the front door which was open.

The joy I felt when I saw my mother standing there in the doorway was phenomenal as relief rushed through my entire body. I thought I was going to pee my pants as I grabbed her and gave a hug, something that I don't do very often. Actually, showing feelings of love or concern in my family isn't something that comes naturally to any of us.

When I finally let her go I could see she had been crying. That was when she told me that my father was dead. I expected her to tell me that he had died of a heart attack or that he had fallen and banged his head hard against the floor or a piece of furniture during one of his heavy drinking sessions. Yet that wasn't how he had expired. The cause of his death was a lamb chop. He had choked to death eating his favourite food.

I nearly laughed out loud. I could actually see him sitting in his favourite chair. He would be surrounded by empty beer cans and overflowing ashtrays. A big plate of chips, lamb chops and eggs would be sitting in front of him and he would be chomping through the mountain of food, scoffing it down like a big, fat, greedy pig. He hardly chewed when he ate and his table manners were disgusting. I ate in a different room from him whenever I could, just so I didn't have to see his revolting antics.

Mum told me that she had gone out to the shops. Dad had needed more beer and she had been sent to get what he needed while he enjoyed his tea. I know he wouldn't have even thanked her for the lovely meal she had prepared for him, before sending her out to get more alcohol to feed his growing addiction.

She had not been gone more than fifteen minutes. When she returned he was lying on the floor in the front room. The table was broken and the dinner plate smashed, food and beer cans littered the floor. His face was bright red and swollen, his eyes and mouth wide open. He was holding his neck, grasping it as he fought for breath. The paramedics had told her that he was dead, beyond help.

I thought she would have been happy, relieved to finally have the chance to live her own life instead of spending her entire waking hours attending to my father's beck and call. Instead she looked devastated. She cried for days and she nearly collapsed at the funeral. She still tells me now how much she misses him and that she will always love him. How sad I think. How pathetic. It's unimaginable to believe that she could hold such affections for another person who emotionally and mentally attacked her for more than twenty years. It's just not right.

I sometimes look at my mum and think what a waste, what a pathetic waste of a human life. In her younger days, she was really pretty. She was very slender, and kind of still is. She had long, jet-black hair which today is kind of more grey than black. She had been very attractive, but years and years of abuse at my father's hand had turned her prematurely old. She was wrinkled and sullen-faced by the age of fifty-five. The amount of red wine she is drinking nowadays isn't helping either.

Anyway, I was glad he was gone. After the undertakers came and took away his body, I went to my room, locked the door and danced a little jig. I did it as quietly as I could so that mum couldn't hear. I also smiled – the biggest and broadest smile ever to grace a person's face since the creation of humankind. I was happier than I had ever been in my life. The bastard was gone.

So, due to the untimely demise of my dad, my walks were put on hold. Mum told me she needed me at home so I took a couple of weeks' holiday and spent it with her. She kept telling me that she needed my support. So, I supported her even though she didn't really give me any support when my dad had viciously teased me about my body, my manner, my lack of backbone and made it clear just how much he wished I wasn't his child.

Come to think of it, she didn't once try to stop dad from hurting me. It never really concerned her that I was being abused.

Even still, I stood by her in her hour of need. I even went with her to the will reading. In fact, I was quite shocked to find out that my father had actually visited a solicitor and had thought about how his family would be taken care of when he was no longer around.

Mum and I were to attend and cousin William, which kind of surprised me. William brought his beautiful girlfriend Hannah with him. She is a real stunner: long blonde hair, big blue eyes, sexy long legs, slender figure and a gorgeous face; she could be a model – one of those supermodels like Kate Moss.

William had always had stunners for girlfriends. He had the looks and the charm to win his way into any girl's pants. Tall with broad shoulders and muscular physique he was the total opposite of me: handsome, rugged good looks, dark hair and bright blue eyes that I envied and despised at the same time.

We all sat together in an old-fashioned, wood-panelled room of the solicitor. The old, bald solicitor dressed in a black suit, white shirt and grey tie read the will, including all the bits that no one was really interested in. Then he finally got to the good bit. Dad had been insured, well insured. He was worth three hundred thousand and he had left one hundred thousand to my mother, one hundred thousand to me and the other one hundred thousand was to go to William. In the will, he referred to William as the son he never had.

I remember turning to look at my mother. I thought she would be upset that my father had left so much money to someone that wasn't even related to him, but she wasn't. In fact, she looked pleased for him and gave his hand a squeeze when he blushed at the thought of being left a huge share of our inheritance.

I knew his blushes were insincere. He didn't care about my mother or me. He was already thinking about how he was going to spend the money. My money! I knew I wouldn't hear the end of this. He would tease me every day at work about my dad and how he thought I was a pathetic excuse of a child. My working life was going to be even more miserable now.

"Wow, I just don't know what to say." William rubbed his face and made it look like he was wiping a tear from his eyes. "Bill was a great man. I am going to miss him so much."

I watched as he turned and gave my mum a big hug and of course she responded in kind.

"He loved you so much, William," my mother wept. "Always remember that."

"I know he did," William replied as he continued to hug my mum. "I just can't believe he is gone."

He looked over to me with a smug expression on his face and winked. He was loving this.

I sat there as long as I could before excusing myself. I ran through the solicitor's office and into the small, unisex toilet. I locked the door before I fell to my knees. I dug my nails into my hands until they bled. I had to. I had to find an outlet, a way to vent my pent-up rage, the anger I had held inside for so long, that up until now I had controlled and tried to ignore.

Now it was spilling free, oozing from every sweaty pore of my body. I closed my eyes and whispered obscenities. I verbally abused my dead dad, my unloving mother and William the arsehole. I hated them all and I wished I had the courage to go back into the solicitor's office and tell them all to go to hell.

Of course, though, I didn't. Instead I got up from the floor, washed the blood from my hands and wet my face before I left the seclusion of the cloakroom.

I looked calm and in control as I met my mother at the bottom of the stairs that led out to Fort William's High Street. I probably looked as if I didn't care that my father had left a huge portion of my inheritance to William. I smiled politely and said goodbye to William and Hannah. They smiled back and were just as pleasant, but they had to be, my mum was there.

As I walked away with my mum I thought about how good it would feel to gut William like a fish. I knew it would bring me instant satisfaction and my working life would be a hundred times better. Maybe with him gone I might even get a promotion. Not that I would ever do anything so awful. It isn't in my nature to hurt someone or something. So, I knew there was only one thing for it. I had to escape. I had to get far, far away from all the people I hate.

Deciding that I was not quite ready for the walk that Sarah had suggested, I instead went for a leisurely stroll through An Torr woodland to the historic Signal Rock. This gentle ramble explores the woodland in the central part of Glencoe. According to Trip Advisor, Signal Rock was where the signal was given to begin the Glencoe Massacre.

I decided to combine the visit to Signal Rock with the Clachaig Flats to make a round trip. So, the next day I set out early, parked my car and got my rucksack out of the boot and checked its contents. I got out my compass and map, and popped a bit of chewing gum into my mouth before checking the time. It was only six in the morning as I headed up the mountain.

I was giddy with excitement and I didn't care about the grey sky or the dark clouds or even the drizzling rain. I had decided not to stay all night; I thought better of it as my mum had been crying all night. I could hear through the bedroom wall and wanted to bang on it to tell her to shut up and get over him. I wished she would wake up to the fact the if she had died before my father that he would not have batted an eyelid. He would not have splashed out on a lavish funeral and casket, or placed her ashes on the fireplace. He would have put her body in a black bag and left it out for the rubbish men. Anyway, that aside I still worry about her, even though she doesn't have any concerns or thoughts for me.

The walk was gentle, a bit too tame for me but I could not complain about the scenery. It was beautiful and it made me thankful for being a Scottish person to be surrounded by such a breathtakingly, stunning landscape and I took tons of pictures. No wonder Americans travel halfway around the world just to visit our villages and towns and to trek over our thistle and heather-clad countryside. As I reached Signal Rock it started to rain heavily, but because most of the walk was through woodland that was thick with huge, tall ferns and spruces, I didn't get very wet. The damp air made the forest smell sweet and fresh and I inhaled deeply to get a lungful of healthy, untainted oxygen. Every now and then I would stop and look up through the trees at the sky above. It made me feel so small being inside this big woodland, with trees towering up and higher and higher into the sky and all around me.

I stood at the Signal Rock plaque and thought about what this location meant to Scottish history. The story goes that a fire was started at five a.m. on the 13th of February 1692 to signal to the soldiers, led by John Graham of Claverhouse, to begin the vicious attack on the MacDonald villages throughout Glencoe. Hundreds of men, women and children died in the Glen.

What a bloodthirsty lot us Scots are, I thought, as I tucked into a cheese and pickle sandwich.

When I reached the Clachaig Flats I realised that I would not be able to camp anyway. The Forestry Commission had put a stop to camping in the area due to people misusing the countryside. Sewage, rubbish, beer cans and liquor bottles were left behind by individuals who had come into the wilderness to party. They probably thought they could get away with misbehaving in the countryside, far away from the cities and towns, but their lack of respect for Mother Nature had ruined it for everyone. Camping was forbidden and the forest rangers carried out routine sweeps of the area to check that no one was breaking the rules. It made me mad to think that people were so insensitive and if I were a forest ranger, I would beat anyone I caught mistreating the countryside to teach them a lesson.

When I got home that night I updated the journal I had started after my first outing to document my walks and ambles through the Scottish countryside. I printed out all the pictures I had taken at the sites I visited. They looked great and I pasted each one into the big, black book and added a few comments next to each one. Once I was finished, I looked through the book again and again. I was hooked and wanted to be back there, back in the forests, the mountains, back in the wilderness.

The next walk I selected was another woodland walk to the historic site of Inveriggan where another thirteen members of the McDonald clan died in the massacre of 1692. While there I paid my respects. Maybe I'm not a descendant of the McDonalds but I am Scottish and proud of my heritage. After all I am a Donaldson and I did a wee bit of research on the family name. Donaldson is a surname related to the great Clan Donald or McDonald. The first chief Donald was the son of Ranald. He was described as a self-styled Lord of the Isles, whatever that means, and the son of a great Norse King.

I like to think I am a direct descendant of Lord Donald. I could see myself as a lord of a huge castle with lots of faithful subjects. I would have a number of beautiful wives who would tend to my every need as I governed my subjects with a strong, powerful hand, making then know who was in charge. I would be a fair lord but also stern. How great would that be.

My next adventure saw me make a long trip to the Angus Glens where I took a leisurely walk up to Corrie Fee. The path that leads to the enclosed Corrie is very popular with locals and tourists alike. The path has been recently upgraded to cater for the thousands of visitors the area receives every year. I know I said I didn't want to go where there are lots of people but I needed to see this place.

Trip Advisor, which as you can tell is where I get a lot of info about the best places to visit, said the valley was created by a glacier during the Ice Age. It is also known for rare plants and wildlife including golden eagles and water voles. Once you are in the valley, it is like you have gone back in time. The area is well looked after and is untainted by modern life.

What I loved about Corrie Fee was the fact that you had to climb over the fence using a wooden ladder. On the other side the valley spreads out with greenery as far as the eye can see. Directly across from where I was standing at the other side of Corrie Fee is a magnificent waterfall. I followed the winding stream to the source and filled my water bottle with pure mountain water. It tasted fantastic and I emptied my reserve bottles and filled them up with the ice-cold liquid so that I could take it home to enjoy over the next few days.

With a month and a half of weekend walking under my belt, I finally felt ready to tackle the more demanding walk that Sarah had suggested. This time though I would be camping out, spending the night under the stars and the week leading up to my planned trip felt like an eternity. All I could think about was getting up the mountain, finding a spot to camp and finally being alone.

Work dragged on and on that week and William was a complete tosser to me every day. On the Wednesday, he threw fish guts across the room when I had my back turned. The gooey, mushy blob landed on my head and I spent nearly an hour trying to wash intestines and blood from my hair.

It wasn't funny but William laughed and laughed for hours. At one point his face went completely red as he laughed so hard it made him cough and I all I could think about was putting my hands around his throat and strangling him. I would laugh as I watched his face turn from red to blue, but of course I could only imagine this. I didn't have the balls or the strength to turn it into reality.

So instead I carried on working with soaking wet hair that smelt of fish inners, and lost myself in the thought that in two days' time I would be back out in the wilds of the Scottish Highlands where nobody would bother or bully me.

CHAPTER THREE

MY FIRST ADVENTURE

Speaking honestly, I found the walk very tiring. I had picked the route that she had mapped out that led up Carn Mor Dearg – a smaller mountain that is attached to the side of Ben Nevis but with an equally demanding and exhilarating route to the top. It is hard to believe that it is one of Scotland's highest mountains because it looks so small standing next to the mighty and majestic Ben Nevis.

I thought I was quite fit. I eat healthily and try to look after my body. I only take the car when I really need to, like if I am going to Inverness to pick up shopping for my mum.

Anyway, I was knackered after two and a half hours of walking so I stopped for a drink and a banana. There is nothing like a banana to help boost your metabolism and raise your energy levels. I sat on a grassy mound and looked out at the stunning scenery. The morning mist hadn't cleared and it lay across the fields like a blanket of cotton wool. In the distance, I could see a farmer. He was tending to a herd of cattle, feeding them, fattening them up and getting them ready for slaughter.

A kestrel or sparrow hawk flew over my head, close enough for me to see its beautiful golden plumage. It hovered overhead for a few moments before swooping down to catch a mouse in its powerful talons. I was wowed by the bird's hunting skills and how easy it found it to pounce on its prey before it ever had any idea that it was in danger.

I wondered how it felt to have such an awesome presence. How it would feel to be so sleek, to be a silent assassin and I visualised myself with wings, with brightly coloured feathers and a huge wingspan. I would silently swoop down on my prey, my antagonists, the people who had abused and used me all my life. They would have no idea I was coming to get them until I plucked them from the ground and carried them off screaming and struggling to get free. Fear would be etched on their faces as they wondered when and how their end would come.

Still smiling I removed the wonderful daydream from my mind and put the banana skin in a bag and then into my rucksack. Getting up again, I started walking. It wasn't long before the walking path split into two and I headed up the one that Sarah had suggested.

My smile turned to a wide toothy grin when I thought about Sarah. What a fox. Anyone would be lucky to have her and I considered visiting her at work in a day or two to let her know that I had taken her suggestion. I was sure she would be happy to see me or at least I hoped so.

I trekked for about another two hours before the pass kind of tapered off into a very thin and narrow footpath that wove around the mountain and in some places, was very close to the edge, so close that I kind of veered off the path and instead took the more tiring option where I had to practically fight my way through thick heather with big, clumping roots. A couple of times I lost my footing and fell face first into the wiry bushes. The first time I fell over I wasn't too pleased and after getting to my feet, I pulled a big clump of the bush out by its roots and threw it over the edge of the mountain. The second time I just kicked the bushes and called them obscenities until my temper calmed down and I felt ready to move on.

After that I didn't mind anytime I fell over again. I had got my anger out and I always feel better when I've let my pent-up emotions out. I didn't really think I had a temper until recently and in some ways, I am glad that I have found that I actually do have some genuine emotions and feelings.

An hour or so later I cleared the green, lushness of the mountain and started to ascend with rock and rubble under foot. My feet didn't really enjoy the new sensation and the fact that they had to work even harder now as the climb became steeper but the rest of me didn't mind a bit. The sun had risen and the sky was clear of rain clouds. It was going to be a glorious spring day.

I had been walking for hours now and only stopping for a drink or an energy bar. Finally, I reached the spot that Sarah had suggested. Most of the landscape was now grey and dreary, and there really wasn't much vegetation around. At first, I thought I had maybe taken the wrong route and for a short while considered turning back and heading down the mountain a bit until I found somewhere I could set up camp for the night.

Then I noticed the path divided again. I had two choices. I could either continue going up or I could carry on a path that would take me around the side of the mountain. Sarah had told me that the camping spot she used was the last area of grassland that was suitable for pitching a tent before the mountain terrain changed, so I knew I wasn't meant to go any further up. So, I decided I would visit the top of Ben Nevis another day.

About ten minutes later I had found the perfect spot. In a cluster of trees, I found a small clearing and sat down. I was a bit out of breath so I lay on the grass for a while, reflecting on the walk and how much I was enjoying my own company. It was great to be away from my mum, William and the fish shop.

Finally, I got up and unpacked my rucksack. I would be lying if I said I found it easy to pitch my tent. Truthfully it took so long that I thought I might be sleeping out in the open. It was about three in the afternoon when I finally had my tent sorted out and my sleeping bag and the other few comforts I had brought with me.

Once I was set up I just stood and listened. I cupped my left ear as I strained to listen to silence. It was so peaceful, so quiet that I felt like I was the only person alive in the entire world. I would love that to happen and for a few moments that thought actually pleased me and I imagined myself running through the streets of Fort William wearing nothing but a pair of green wellies and singing my favourite rock songs at the top of my voice.

As the evening ascended and the light began to fade, I found large rock to hide behind where I dug a small hole and squatted down and tried to empty my bowels. It was at that point that I heard voices. Two women were heading my way and by the sound of things they were nearby and getting closer. I remember how quickly I managed to pull up my underwear and trousers before they came into sight.

I couldn't believe my eyes. It was Sarah, with another girl who wasn't nearly as attractive as the beautiful Sarah. They were giggling and happy. Sarah was dressed in long, grey-coloured shorts and a black and white striped T-shirt. Her short, blonde-haired, skinny friend wore the same coloured trousers but had on a bright pink T-shirt that was nearly as loud as her laugh.

Sarah smiled when she saw me and whispered something into her friend's ear. She said something that made her laugh even louder. I remember how it made me feel, seeing her. My legs turned to jelly, my stomach churned and my heart skipped a beat or two. I knew I had fallen for her and in a big way.

"So, you took my advice," Sarah said. She was smiling and making me weak at the knees. All I could do was smile back and nod. "What do you think of the area? Isn't it just lovely?"

Again, all I could do was smile and nod. It was pathetic really.

Her friend had obviously realised that I had a thing for Sarah. It made her extremely giggly and very annoying. She was no way as pretty as Sarah. She was blonde, dirty blonde and slender with tiny breasts. She did have pretty eyes but a rather big nose and teeth that I just didn't find attractive at all. Her name was Laura and she also worked at the visitor centre.

Sarah and her stupid, giggly friend chatted with me for only a few minutes before they headed off up the mountain. We chatted about the weather, about the camping spot and she gave me a tip or two on the best spots to birdwatch. Not that I had listened much to what she had said. She was the only bird I wanted to watch. I couldn't stop thinking about her and the fact that she was here on the mountain at the same time as me. Surely that had to mean something?

After Sarah left I thought of all the things that I had wanted to say to her, that hadn't managed to enter my mind or mouth during our brief encounter. I wanted to tell her how pretty she was, how her beautiful red hair looked so much better when she wore it down, allowing it to hang loosely around her shoulders.

I found myself whispering her name over and over again. I could not help myself. I just could not stop thinking about her and when I returned to the spot where I intended to relieve myself, I found myself doing something else behind the privacy of the rocks.

Later that night when it was dark, I got out my radio and wound it up. I found a station that played rock music from morning to night and then I lit the campfire. I made sausages, bacon and two eggs. It tasted magnificent. For some reason eating out in the wilderness made food a lot taster and I could have eaten the same again if I had the room.

Feeling stuffed, I lay back on the grass and looked at the sky above. It was beautiful and I studied the stars for an age, trying to find and name all the constellations. When I finally grew bored, I got to my feet just as one of my favourite rock songs started. It was Bon Jovi and I sang along to 'Livin' on a Prayer' at the top of my voice as I danced around the campfire. I must have looked like a complete idiot but I did not care. I was having the time of my life. I was alone, doing the things I like and there was nobody about to ridicule or harass me. I did not think life could get any better.

I got so into the moment that I stripped off. I took off every stitch of clothing and whooped and shouted as I danced and jumped around the campfire in my birthday suit. I felt like a prehistoric man, a caveman who had just discovered fire and was celebrating the prospect of never being cold again.

Finally, I started to feel cold and thought it was probably best to settle down for the night. My sleeping bag was already set out and I put my shirt and pants back on before hitting the sack. Of course, I put out the campfire before I retired.

As I lay in my tent in the pitch dark, I actually found myself a bit frightened, to begin with anyway. There was hardly a sound. Every now and then a breeze would make the trees overhead rustle and I think I heard an owl or other bird of the night call out in the darkness. A twig snapped next to my tent and it made me jump up with fright. I nervously unzipped the tent and was relieved to see a couple of birds digging around the campsite looking for scraps. They flew off when they realised they had company.

I zipped up the tent again and lay down. I giggled as I thought of my girlish behaviour. Who did I think was going to be outside the tent, Freddy Kruger or the Boogie Man? That was the first and last time I was afraid of the dark. From then on, the darkness and silence of the night-time would be a time for thinking, when I pondered my life and made decisions about my future.

The next day I awoke feeling refreshed and invigorated. It was the best night's sleep I had ever had in my entire pathetic life and I checked my watch. It was nearly ten in the morning and I never sleep that late. I could not believe it. I had actually managed to sleep the entire night and nearly most the morning without waking once.

I finally got up and instantly felt sad. I had to go home. I had to leave soon. I promised my mum I would be back sometime in the afternoon. She wanted me home; she wanted me to be there to keep her company again and I was getting fed up of being her shoulder to lean on every time she wanted to cry or talk about my dad.

Anyway, being the diligent son that I am, I ate a couple of energy bars, packed up my camp and headed home. I took a meandering walk home, stopping every now and then to take a photograph, or to check out the wild flowers, or to peer through my binoculars to watch a bird fly overhead just in case it was a rare bird of prey.

I did not mention this before but sometimes I pick a few wild flowers to take home. I search for information on the flower on the internet and I add the information into my journal before I press the flower. I know it is not very manly but I like doing it. I like keeping a memento of my mountain trips.

Anyway, that day I got home and William was there, sitting in my late dad's seat. He was even sitting the way my dad did, legs open, slouched down and my mum had given him a beer which was sitting on the table next to him.

It was like déjà vu. It was like my father had been reincarnated and had come home to make my life miserable for goodness knows how many years. Then again it did not take my dad to be home for my life to be full of bullying. William had taken over from him. Not so much taken over, he had just upped his game, added my dad's share of nastiness to his and now my working life was twice as bad as it was before.

I stood in the doorway as I watched my mum and he converse. She was laughing at his pathetic jokes, hanging on to every word, fuelling his overactive ego. When she finally noticed I was there, her smile vanished and she looked annoyed. She got to her feet and started shouting at the top of her voice. She was mad, really upset.

"Why the hell do you need to be borrowing money from William?" she shouted at me, her face contorted with anger. "You never go out, you never spend any money. So, what the hell are you doing with it?"

William looked up at me, from my father's old chair. He was smirking wickedly, loving the moment and he knew if I called him a liar, my mum would never believe me.

"I think he has been gambling a bit too much. He isn't very good at it either by the sounds of things. I do try to stop him going down to the bookies but he won't listen to me," William said, lying his pants off with every word that came out of his mouth.

"You have a gambling problem!" The shocked look on my mother's face must have been the exact same look that I had.

I tried to tell her no, but she didn't listen.

"If I hear from William that you have been back to the bookies again, I will make sure you never receive your share of the inheritance money. I will make sure William gets your share too."

That made me livid. William was already getting a share of my money and, if he continued to tell lies about me, he could end up with two thirds of the inheritance.

She kept telling me that I should never have taken money from William. That it was wrong to borrow money and the fact that I would not pay him back was embarrassing. I made her feel embarrassed. What a joke.

Her anger, her words were totally unexpected and I took a step back, out of the room as I looked over at William. Mum had her back to him; she could not see the faces he was making or the rude gestures he was making with his hands that were directed at her. He loved every minute of it, loved watching the havoc he was causing.

My mum ordered me to go up to my room and get the three hundred I had borrowed and give it back to William. Of course, William tried to say that the money did not matter but that he had told her about me borrowing the money because he was concerned about my finances and possible gambling addiction.

What a lot of crap! I watched my mum thank him for his concerns and then she forced me to say sorry to William. I was livid! Filled with hate and rage I stamped all the way up the stairs and got the money. I had never borrowed a penny from him. William owed me money and it was a lot more than three hundred pounds. Whenever he asked for money I always gave it to him. Even though I wanted to say no, I just could not, partly because I am a wimp but mostly because I am scared that he will kick the crap out of me if I don't give him what he wants.

So basically, William visiting my mum and causing this trouble was nothing but out of sheer badness.

The next day at work I found out that his father had seen William bullying me. He had been disgusted with William's behaviour and had taken back the car he had just bought for him. William had been livid and to get back at me, he had lied to my mum. He blamed me for the loss of the car. He just could not see that he had brought it on himself.

He had wanted me to look as much of a loser to my mum as he looked to his dad. Mr McGregor knew his only son was a complete and utter loser but he turned a blind eye to his antics most of the time. So, William became a bigger ass with every day. It was only a matter of time before he ended up in jail on an assault or murder charge and if I didn't watch out, with the way he looked at me and treated me, I was very likely to become the person he seriously abused or killed.

CHAPTER FOUR

WILLIAM HAD TO GO

The next day I awoke feeling sad and grumpy. I was miserable from the moment I opened my eyes. I had loved every minute I had spent on Ben Nevis and now I had to return to everyday life. I dressed in jeans, white trainers and a green T-shirt with the big fish motif that was circled with the words 'McGregor's Fresh Fish'. Across the back are the words 'Simply the Best' printed in bright red letters. The T-shirt looks so tacky and stupid but I wouldn't dare tell my boss what I think.

My mum had washed my white overall and I collected it from the kitchen table before heading for work. It only took me ten minutes to get there by foot and as usual I was the first to arrive after Tam McGregor.

I started work straight away. We are always busy right from morning till night and sometimes I only have time to stop to go to the bathroom. William, on the other hand, spends most of the day at the rear of the shop, wheeling and dealing and chatting to his mates.

I often hear them speaking about me. They call me names like freak, weirdo and gender bender. I hate his mates and I hate him too. William treats me like dirt. He pretends to be my friend and knows how to manipulate me into doing things that any sane person would instantly know was going to make them look stupid.

For example, six months ago William and I were speaking about our bodies. He was prancing around the office, flexing his muscles and making me feel really, really jealous. He knows how much I try to bulk up and that no matter how hard I work out and try to keep fit, I just can't make my muscles look any bigger.

I was beginning to get really peed off with him, when he stopped and told me his secret to a great body. He told me that he ate twenty raw fish eyes a day. I told him I didn't believe him so he cut a head off a fish and popped the trout's eyes out. He placed the two black, staring eyes in the palm of his hand.

"Fish eyes are the secret to having a great body like mine." He rolled the fish eyes in the palm of his hand. The sight repulsed me a bit. "They are full of vitamins and minerals that cause a reaction in your muscles. I hardly have to work-out now. These beauties make looking great so easy."

William flexed his chest muscles. His tight-fitting T-shirt helped show off his perfect six pack.

I looked again at the fish eyes and kind of squirmed at the thought of swallowing them. William then quickly popped them into his mouth before washing them down with a swig of orange juice.

Of course, he hadn't really. With a slight of hand trick, the kind that is used by children's entertainers and magicians, he had dropped the fish eyes into a cup without me even noticing. At the time, I was so impressed and so excited that William had actually confided in me and was willing to help me get the muscles I so longed for.

Later that day, I picked ten fish heads that had the biggest, brightest eyes. I popped the eyes and put them into my empty sandwich box. I couldn't wait to get home and swallow them down. All I could think about was waking up the next day with bulging biceps. I imagined myself walking down the high street, the sleeves of my T-shirt ripping open as I flexed my muscles for the hordes of sexy women who couldn't keep their eyes or hands off me.

Of course, that didn't happen. I got home with the fish eyes and before I had time to put them in the fridge, my mum had asked me to run an errand. Of course, I did as she asked and got the shopping, went to the bank and picked up my dad from the pub.

Finally, when I got home and opened the box, the fish eyes didn't look as enticing as they did earlier.

They didn't smell so good either. In fact, when I opened them I had to stand back as the smell was really overpowering and made me feel sick.

Yet that didn't stop me from eating them. I just couldn't stop thinking about the change of having big, manly muscles and, with one hand pinching my nose, I downed them as quickly as I could. Once they were all gone I drank a can of coke to take away the nasty taste. It didn't work but that was the least of my worries.

Two hours later I was curled up in the foetal position, clutching my stomach and moaning and groaning in pain.

My stomach ached so bad that at one point I thought I would have to crawl downstairs and ask my mum to take me to the hospital. I felt as if I needed my stomach pumped before it exploded.

Just as I thought the pain couldn't get any worse, my stomach starts to churn and make loud, gurgling noises, so loud that I thought my parents could hear the awful sounds downstairs. I was sweating buckets and I felt faint. Then the nausea came and, as I crawled to the toilet down the hall, I had to gag back the sick that was already coming up my throat.

I barely made it to the toilet when everything I had eaten that day forced its way out of my mouth at a furious pace. Dark coloured water with different coloured chunks flooded the white toilet bowl, staining it a dirty brown colour.

When I could wretch no more I lay down on the bathroom floor, trying to get as far away as possible from the foul smelling sick. I felt weak but relieved that I was no longer in pain. The cramps were gone but my stomach still gurgled and I knew I was going to have a terrible bout of the bottom squirts very soon.

Finally, I mustered up the strength to get off the floor and returned to the toilet to flush away the vomit and clean up the mess I had made. I looked down into the bowl as I flushed. Twenty black eyes stared back up at me, glimmering brightly, mocking me and laughing at me for my foolish behaviour.

That was the day I realised just how much of an evil swine William could be. I lay in my bed that night, tears streaming from my eyes as I tried to cry as quietly as possible. I felt so ashamed that I had allowed vanity to cloud my mind so much that I could not see that William wanted to hurt me and make me look even more stupid than I already did to his friends. I knew that the next morning they would all be waiting for me at the back of the shop and they were.

I had planned to call in sick but I knew if I did that I would be just postponing the inevitable. As I opened the backdoor to allow the delivery man access, I heard the laughing and jeering. William and about seven of his mates were standing there, they were all holding fish heads, the ones I had taken the eyes from, and posing, flexing their muscles as they mocked and bullied me.

"How were your fish eyes, Billy?" William laughed as he held up in the air one of the fish heads with missing eyes.

His mates were just as fit and muscular as William. They were also just as vulgar, nasty and stupid as him.

"Look at your muscles, man," one of his mates shouted. "You look just like a body builder."

"Take your top off, show us your pecs," another boy shouted.

They were all laughing at me, taunting me.

As I turned to go back into the shop, they started throwing the fish heads, most of them battering off the back of my head. The fish heads didn't hurt, they were soft and mushy and some of the fish scales got mangled into my hair, making it look greasy, dirty and wet.

So, what did I do about it? Did I retaliate? Did I fight back? Did I hell! I did what I always did, I took it. I let them walk all over me, laugh at me and abuse me. I even picked up the fish heads. That's just how pathetic I am – or was until that morning.

I got into work, put on my overalls and started to gut the fish. I'm an expert gutter now and my boss often commends me for my excellent filleting. I had been working no more than half an hour when William came in the back door. He looked awful, like he had a really bad hangover and he reeked of alcohol.

I pretended not to notice his state and carried on working. William took a seat in the corner and opened a can of juice and started to read the morning newspaper. He looked slightly annoyed, and kept looking over at me as if my presence was not welcome.

Finally, he spoke. He asked me how my trip was. I replied with a few words, telling him it was okay and that was about it. For what felt like a long time, William kept staring at me. Then he asked me about my inheritance money, if I had plans for it, if I knew what I was going to spend the money on. I just shrugged my shoulders and carried on working. I didn't want to speak about the money. I didn't want to be reminded that my father had left him a huge share of my inheritance.

William did not like my lack of interest in his conversation. He got to his feet and walked over to where I was standing. I turned to look at him. He is everything I am not: tall, dark, handsome, muscular, witty and smart mouthed. He could have any woman he wanted in Fort William and probably anywhere in Scotland.

He smiled at me. It was one of his dark, sneaky smiles that made me worried whenever I saw one grace his handsome face. Then he told me what he was going to do with his money – what he was going to do with my money.

First of all, he was going to buy Hannah an engagement ring. Nothing too fancy or expensive, he was only buying it to shut her up so that he could go on holiday with his friends. He was taking his buddies to Amsterdam for a week. He called it a sex, beer and dope fest where they would party from morning to night and shag as many women as they could. The man that screwed the most women would win a prize at the end of the week.

I felt disgusted. I couldn't believe that he would be getting engaged one day and then cheat on his new fiancée the next. He really was a creep. A low life that made even my dad look good. He had no respect for women, no scruples and had never ever felt guilt or remorse. I hated him. I hated him so much that it took all my strength to not put the knife I held through his cold, unfeeling heart.

That was when I knew I had to do something about him. I had to stop him from getting his hands on my money and using it to satisfy his sick, sexual fantasies. So, I pretended to be interested in what he was saying and told him that I did not plan to spend the money yet. That I was going to save it. I told him that I would keep some in the bank and the rest I would put into my money box that I kept under my bed. I told him I already kept my wages in the money box.

His eyes lit up when I said I had money hidden in my house. He could not hide his interest. He even asked me how much money I had in the money box. I told him the truth: twelve thousand and sixty-six pounds.

I knew this because I had counted it on Friday night just before I had packed for my trip. William smiled and put his arm around my shoulder. I knew he was going to ask me if I would lend him some money. He often asked me to lend him some cash but usually it was a tenner or a fiver. He always promised to pay it back but I have never seen one penny in return.

I asked him how much and watched as he released me from his grip and walked over to the other side of the room. I knew he was thinking, plotting, getting a story together to try and make me believe that he really needed the money.

Then the lies flowed out of his mouth, a river of untruths so deep that I was surprised that he didn't drown in his deceitful words. He told me that if I lent him two thousand pounds that he could buy a beautiful ring for Hannah. He knew that I was a sucker for her and that I would do anything to please her. He knew how I felt about her, how I wanted her.

I let him finish, pretending to be interested in his plight and of course I agreed to lend him the money, but there was a catch, this time he had to do something for me.

At first, I did not think he would agree to my terms but finally he gave in when I said I would lend him an extra thousand pounds. I even told him he could have five hundred pounds up front if he agreed to go hill walking with me at the weekend. I told him that my mum wanted us to spend more time together, which of course was a complete lie. She really liked William but she didn't like his friends and did not want me to have anything to do with them.

I told him I did not want his friends coming along as I did not think they would appreciate the countryside. I told him not to tell anyone that he was spending the day with me, which of course he totally agreed with. No doubt he was worried about what his friends would say if they found out that he was spending time with the weirdo that worked for his father.

I knew that he wouldn't be able to say no to the extra cash and I knew the second I handed over the five hundred pounds that he would run to the travel agents to put down a deposit on the trip to Amsterdam.

He agreed and patted me on the back as I told him I would bring the five hundred pounds in the next day –

which I did. I gave him the money and just as I thought he booked the holiday and bought a packet of cigarettes and six tins of cheap lager with the remaining few pounds.

For the rest of the week I plotted and planned. I knew I had to deal with William; he had to go. He wasn't worthy of Hannah and he did not deserve a share of my inheritance. Yes – there was no doubt in my mind that he was the son my dad had always wanted, and that was what made me despise him even more.

Saturday morning came around quickly and I arranged to meet William at the edge of town at five thirty in the morning. I picked him up on a lonely, quiet and rarely used country lane. I did think about us meeting at the shop as only the Saturday boy and Mr McGregor work the weekend shifts and don't usually arrive until seven, but I couldn't risk us being spotted together. It wasn't part of the plan.

William got into the car. He was still drunk from the night before and wearing designer jeans, a denim jacket, red T-shirt and new white trainers. He was grumpy and swore a few times about how he wished he was in bed instead of out in the cold.

I just ignored him and drove the car into the car park at the base of Ben Nevis. It was deserted – thank goodness. I got my kit out of the boot and gave William a jacket, a black nondescript parka jacket, that wasn't his usual style, but it was a cold morning and for probably the first time in his life, practicality came before fashion.

He put the jacket on and put the hood up, as if he were hiding away inside the jacket in case someone recognised him. Even here with no one to see, he was embarrassed to be with me.

I did not give him a chance to change his mind about the walk ahead. I started off and after a few more swear words, William finally followed. We walked for an hour or so and I stopped to give him a drink, which he really needed and he thanked me.

We walked again for another hour, neither of us speaking until we reached where the road split into two. I stopped and gave William an energy bar and another drink. While he ate I took out my binoculars and focused on the car park below. It was still empty.

William finished his energy bar and threw the wrapper on the ground. Of course, I picked it up and he laughed at me. He called me an idiot and, shortly after we started walking again, the moaning and complaining began.

First it was his feet, then he was cold, then he had a sore head and finally he sat down and refused to walk any further. I knew then that I would have to up the stakes and I offered him another five hundred pounds if he would just finish the walk. I promised him it wasn't much further and the combination of the bribe and the news that he would be able to have a long rest soon, seemed to jerk life back into his body and his attitude instantly changed. He was up and off at a pace that I found it difficult to keep up. Not that I told him that; it would have given him something else to boast about.

Finally, we reached the spot, the spot that Sarah had suggested and where we had met briefly just a week ago. I would have thought about her a lot if I were alone on the mountain, but today I had other things on my mind and a job to do.

William sat down between the trees and took off his now very dirty trainers and socks. He had blisters on both of his heels and I had to stop myself from smirking when he groaned at the pain when he burst them. Goo ran down his heels and he rubbed the back of his feet in the grass before putting his shoes and socks back on.

I could tell he was eager to get back down the mountain. He had played his part and now he wanted his money. So, I knew I had to act there and then.

Taking a silver flask from my rucksack I offered William a drink of rum. I knew he wouldn't refuse a tipple. It did not matter if it was a spirit, a liqueur or a lager. William would never say no if he knew that he could get pissed.

He practically grabbed the bottle from my hand. He held it up in front of my face and said something that sounded Russian, which probably meant 'down the hatch' or 'bottoms up' or maybe even something obscene.

It took him all of thirty seconds before the bottle was empty. I asked him if he would like another drink and of course he did not refuse. So, I took the remainder of the half bottle of rum out of my rucksack and passed him the bottle.

William unscrewed the cap and before he put the bottle to his lips asked me if I wanted a drink. I refused. I didn't want to go to sleep.

"You are so pathetic," William said, his words a bit slurry already. "You won't even have a drink. You scared you might like it too much and turn into a drunken slob, just like your loser of a dad?"

He laughed at that comment; he thought he was so funny. He had no idea I was about to have the last laugh.

I watched as he chugged on the bottle. He was the one that seemed to have a drinking problem, and made him more like my late dad. He continued to drink and it wasn't long before he started to speak a lot of rubbish and tell truths he would not usually be so ready to share with me.

He started to tell me about Hannah. He told me he did not really love her.

"Bet you wish you could find a girl like Hannah," he smirked. "I watch the way you look at her."

He took another swig from the bottle. "She really is sexy and the sex, you could never imagine how good it is. She is game for anything. Some of the things she had let me do to her, I reckon they could be illegal."

He started laughing uncontrollably and then started giving me full details on what exactly he had done to her. He was disgusting and depraved.

She wasn't really his type and the only reason he stayed with her was because of the sex. He laughed when I blushed. He knew he was making me feel uncomfortable. I did not want to know about his intimate life.

William then started to yawn. The sleeping pills were working. I had added thirty sleeping pills to the bottle of rum and I knew it would not take long for them to start working. I had stolen them from my mum's huge stockpile of drugs that she kept in the bathroom cabinet.

William shook his head. He was obviously finding it hard to focus and he looked at me, or at least tried to, and told me that he wanted to go home.

I pretended to agree that we should start to head down the mountain and watched as William tried to get to his feet. It was so funny that I couldn't stop myself from giggling out loud. He was staggering and falling over onto his knees. He could only stay standing for a second or so before he lost balance again and fell over.

I knew then that he wasn't going anywhere and I got to work. I left him trying to get up and walked over to an area at the back of the cluster of trees. The ground was soft here, a bit marshy in places and I had a spade in my rucksack which I took out and started to dig.

First of all, I removed the grass and turf. I would need this again. I then started to dig a hole, one big enough to fit William's body. It took me about two hours to dig the hole and I had a lot of blisters on my hand by the time I was finished. Sweating profusely and covered in mud and muck, I went and checked on William.

He was lying face down on the grass and his nose was bleeding from hitting his face hard on the ground as he finally passed out. I checked for a pulse on his neck and there was a faint one. I then removed the coat he was wearing. It was mine after all and I probably would need it again, besides my late grandma had bought me the coat.

William was a lot heavier that he looked and I found it hard to drag his body to the hole. I had to take several breaks but finally I managed to push him over the side and he fell into the ground. He was at least four feet down and he looked kind of small and pathetic.

I stared at him for a while, wondering if he saw this coming; if he knew that one day I would pay him back for the years of abuse I had to endure at his hand.

I said a small prayer for him before I started to shovel the earth back in.

I am pretty sure he was still breathing when I put him in the ground but I doubted he was still alive when I had filled the hole and put the grass and turf back. I stamped on the ground as hard as I could so that it looked level and flat. I had to make sure that it did not look as if it had been disturbed. People would be passing-by here, maybe even stopping.

I inspected the ground thoroughly and took a seat on the grass next to where William lay. I waited and waited for what felt like an age, staring patiently at the spot. I wanted to make sure that he couldn't get out, that he didn't get out. I had horrible images of his hands breaking through the surface and I held the spade tightly, just in case I had to beat him around the head and back down into the ground.

Finally, when I was satisfied that he wasn't coming back, I started to remove the evidence. I found the empty rum bottle close to where I found William. I put the lid back on and put it back in my rucksack with my spade.

Before setting off back down the mountain I contemplated heading up to the summit. This would be the last time I would visit Carn Mor Dearg.

It was best if I didn't come back and the thought of never seeing a sunset or sunrise from the top of the mountain filled me with sadness. Yet I knew I couldn't go to the top today, not when I am carrying a coat, a spade and the murder evidence in my bag. So instead I went home.

Back at the house I put the hip flask and rum bottle in the bin and put the coat I had loaned to William in the washing machine. Then I ate dinner with my mum – I think it was steak and chips followed with apple pie. She asked me about my walk and I told her I had gone to Lochaber for a short hill walk.

That night I lay in bed and thought about what I had done. I tried to feel remorseful and guilty but was unable to feel anything but elation. William was gone. I would hopefully get his share of the inheritance money back and Hannah could find a boyfriend who actually cared about her. With those thoughts on my mind I fell asleep with a smile on my face.

The following Monday I went to work. I started early, but not too early to arouse suspicion but I knew if I didn't work extra hard that it would be a very long working day and I did not want to stay late as there was a programme on river fishing that I did not wish to miss, one of the few television programmes I do enjoy. I was thinking of taking up fishing. I was thinking of buying a rod.

About ten in the morning Hannah came into the shop asking to speak to Mr McGregor. She looked awful: her eyes were all red and puffy and she had obviously been crying for a long time.

Mr McGregor and Hannah talked for about ten minutes and then she came into the back of the shop. I did not like to see her looking so distressed but I knew that the pain she felt now would be short lived, and when she had forgotten about William and found a new boyfriend that she would soon be happy again.

She asked me if I had seen William. I told her I had not seen him since Friday, just before we closed the shop at the end of the working day. She told me that they had gone out on Friday night.

Hannah looked hellish. Her usually flawless makeup was patchy and streaky from all the tears she had been crying.

"We had a terrible fight," she confided as she dabbed the tears from her eyes with a hankie. "He sent me home. Said he wanted to stay out with his mates, so gave me some money for the taxi and went off with his friends without even saying goodbye."

She started to really sob. "He told me he might not be home until sometime Saturday. He had a business deal to take care of that meant he could finally buy me an engagement ring."

I suggested that maybe his business deal took longer that he thought. That was when she started to sob even louder.

"I phoned all his friends yesterday when he didn't come home. I asked them if they knew where he might be. A couple said something about him going up Ben Nevis for a walk. Can you ever imagine William going for a walk in the hills?" she continued. "It doesn't sound right. William doesn't walk anywhere if he doesn't have to. It just doesn't make sense."

I nearly dropped my filleting knife. William had blabbed. He was meant to keep his big mouth shut but he could not keep his gob shut.

Luckily, he had not mentioned my name but I wondered how long it would take for Hannah to figure out that he was doing business with me and that we had gone for a walk together.

She asked me if I knew anything about the business deal William had mentioned. I told her no. I did not know what else to say, so I thought it was best to say as little as possible just in case I put my foot in it and said something that might raise her suspicions.

She was still crying when she left and to tell you the truth I was not really concerned about her. I was more worried about her telling someone else about what she knew. What if she went to the police or told Mr McGregor. It was obvious - Hannah would have to be silenced if she asked any more questions.

So, I knew I would have to do something and I had already planned for this probability. I had mailed a letter from Inverness on Sunday morning. It was from William and I was an ace at copying his handwriting. It was not hard to do. A five-year-old child could write better than William. The letter address to Hannah was very vague. It explained his absence and informed her that he would be back in a week or so. The business deal had not gone to plan and clinching the deal was taking a lot longer that he expected.

William was well known for his wheeling and dealing in Fort William. He had sold everything from stolen fish to drugs. He used the money to buy alcohol, hash for personal use and girls. He would often take off for a few days down to London where he paid prostitutes for sex.

Hannah brought the letter into the shop on Tuesday morning and showed it to Mr McGregor. I watched as he read it before he shrugged his shoulders. He was not the least bit concerned for his son. He told her not to worry and that William would come home when he was ready to come home.

I stifled a laugh and got back to work as Hannah left the shop looking slightly annoyed. Nobody was worried about William except her and, as long as that lasted, I would have nothing to worry about.

CHAPTER FIVE

SARAH MADE A FOOL OF ME

It had been a week since anyone had seen William and to celebrate a great, abuse-free week at work, I asked for a half day and finished at noon on Friday. I had plans and I rushed home, had a shower, applied some aftershave and got dressed up.

I was going to see Sarah and I was going to ask her to go hill walking with me. I was a bit nervous; actually, I felt like wetting my pants and there was tightness in my throat – usually a sign that I might be on the way to having a panic attack. This time though I liked the feeling. It wasn't because I was being bullied; it was for all the right reasons – LOVE.

I couldn't wait to see her and I even knew where I was going to take her. We would visit the Lost Valley where the McDonalds clan hid their cattle from other clans to stop it being stolen and was a refuge for escaping clan's folk after the infamous Massacre of

Glencoe. I had researched the valley including the history of the area and planned to 'WOW' Sarah with my knowledge.

So off I went, all dressed up and smelling great. I parked my car outside the visitor centre and got out before I had time to think about what I was doing. I marched right into the empty centre and right up to Sarah who was washing a display stand at the back of the room. All the leaflets that were held on the stand were sitting in neat piles on the floor, the same type of leaflet in each stack.

Before I could chicken out, I just blurted it out. My words came out fast and jumbled and I knew by the strange expression on her face that she was shocked to see me. Once I had finished I took a step back as I knew I was kind of invading her comfort zone as I was just about standing on her feet. When I come to think of it, she did actually have pretty big feet for a woman.

She blushed and dropped the cloth she was holding into a bucket of grey water. The water splashed everywhere, down the sides of the green bucket and on the wooden floor. Her white T-shirt and pale pink three-quarter length trousers were dotted with dirty water marks: she must have been cleaning for some time.

Picking up the bucket she asked me if I would wait outside so that she could speak to me alone. I was not sure if she was embarrassed or if she was thrilled with my date proposal. So, I went outside and sat on the bonnet of my car and waited for her.

It was not long before she came to join me. She smiled and twisted her ponytail, playing with it in a flirty, seductive way, as if she was teasing me. I liked it a lot. I told her more about my plans and about us visiting the Lost Valley. I even suggested that we head up there at the weekend. She told me that she would love to go with me but that she was busy at the weekend but asked if I would be available during the week. Her day off was Tuesday and she suggested that I head to the valley on my own Monday night, pitch the tent and get ready for her arrival early Tuesday morning.

"Do you know how to get to the valley?" she asked me as she continued to play with her hair. Her voice sounded sexy and I felt aroused.

She took a step nearer to me and I could feel my pulse race. I was so in to her. I so wanted her.

I confirmed I knew where she wanted to meet and that I would do as she asked and get set up Monday night. I wanted to go immediately to see Mr McGregor and ask for some holiday days. If I didn't get the days, I would take a sickie. No way I was missing out on a date with Sarah, and I had the feeling that the date would involve a lot more than just hand holding and light kissing; after all she wanted to spend the night. She wanted to be with me. Finally, someone wanted me and liked me.

I was so happy that I nearly yelled out loud with joy. I felt as if I had just won the lottery, and just when I did not think that she could say anything to make the day more perfect, Sarah leant forward, her big, round breasts pressed against my chest as she whispered in my ear.

"I am going to bring my skimpiest nightdress and I will model it for you on Tuesday night, just before I allow you to undress me. In case you don't know, I won't be wearing anything underneath. I know a wild, country boy like you loves going commando."

With my jaw hanging wide open she kissed me on the cheek before heading back into the visitor centre. Finally, I managed to remove my horny ass from the bonnet of the car and headed home.

I think I grinned the rest of the day and was still smiling when I went shopping for a new, big, luxurious, two-man tent, a double blow-up mattress and a double sleeping bag. I got a luxury, double sleeping bag that cost nearly a hundred pounds but I knew Sarah was worth it. I spent another hundred pounds on a hamper basket which contained fine dining dinner plates and crystal glasses. I wanted us to have an extra special dinner on Tuesday night. I had pictured us sitting close together, my arm around her shoulder as we sipped fine champagne. Above us would be the black sky that would be lit by the stars and moon. All around us would be silence and open countryside and there would be no one to bother us as I finally made my move and seduced her. I would no longer be a virgin and that thought filled me with elation and, I kind of wished that William was still about so that I could tell him that he could no longer slag me off about my non-existent sex life.

I bought the champagne and other goodies from a posh-nosh shop in Inverness. Then I posted another letter to Hannah. I had to keep her at bay for another week or so. I did not want her bothering me next week, so to ensure this, I took the week off. Mr McGregor was not too happy to be giving me a holiday but since I had not taken a full week off since June the year before, he had no choice but to let me go.

With the spare time on my hands, I spent Sunday packing and repacking my rucksack and the hamper, except for the perishables; they would go into the hamper on Monday. I couldn't settle and I had to find things to do around the house to keep me busy. I checked the oil in my car, washed it and then washed it again. I pressed my hiking trousers and shirt at least three times and picked the underpants I was going to wear at least six times before I finally decided to go into town and buy some new ones. I bought three pairs of designer, Calvin Klein jersey shorts that were tight fitting and made me look quite sexy – or so I thought.

At noon on Monday I reversed out of the driveway and headed for Glencoe. At this time of year, off peak season, there would be very little visitors to Glencoe and the Lost Valley, especially during the week. The thought of the seclusion pleased me and I fantasised about my alone time with Sarah as I parked the car and got the hamper and my rucksack from the boot.

I can't tell you the thoughts I was having; they were rather rude but, if it all happened as planned, I would be smiling and singing happy songs for a year, maybe even longer. I couldn't wait to get my hands on her.

My rucksack was very heavy and the hamper wasn't very light in weight either. I started off in the direction of the valley, taking my time and taking rests whenever I needed them. Within half an hour I was totally knackered and I had to keep telling myself that it was worth it – Sarah was worth it.

According to one of the websites I had looked at, it should take a fit person an hour and a half to make a return trip to the Lost Valley and back to the car park. I doubted that their figures included a person carrying a heavy rucksack and a hamper filled with champagne, food, china and crystal.

It took me three hours to get to where I wanted to be and as I entered the valley I paused to take in the breathtaking, unspoiled scenery. It was quite something. Green, lush land surrounded me and I looked up to the top of the dark, craggy, rocky hills and wondered if I would ever have the balls to start hill climbing and mountaineering.

I walked through the valley for about ten minutes and stopped when I came to a large rock that was kind of round in shape and I wondered if it had rolled from the top of one of the mountains down into the valley floor below. There was also a river nearby and I could hear the rhythmic, trickling of water and knew that the sound would be the only one I would probably hear in the dead of night.

I thought this would be the perfect place to make camp and I gently put down the hamper before taking off the heavy rucksack. My shoulders ached and I rubbed them before getting to work. I had a campsite to prepare. It had to be perfect for Sarah.

Setting up the tent, I inflated the navy, double mattress with the nifty, battery-operated device that came with it and spent what seemed like an age positioning it in the tent. I wanted everything to be perfect – every last little detail had to be right. Once the tent was sorted I headed down to the burn with the bucket I had brought for chilling the champagne.

The sun was starting to go down and the orange glow in the sky reflected on the surrounding countryside creating weird and wonderful rust-coloured shadows. I took a seat on the ground next to the burn and even though it was a bit nippy I took my hiking boots and socks off and put my feet in the freezing cold, fresh water. I cringed at the coldness and pulled my feet out after a few moments. Even though it had soothed my sore, aching feet I did not think the coldness would be very good for my circulation and if I left them in the water much longer my feet might have turned blue.

As I put my socks and boots back on, I found myself contemplating life. I actually found myself thinking about my mum and dad. I wondered what my life would have been like if I had normal parents, ones like the other kids I went to school with, ones like William's.

I imagined myself coming home from school. Dinner would be cooking and it would smell delicious.

A lovingly prepared dinner, one of my mum's many mouth-watering recipes, from her own created cookbook of our favourite meals. My mum would be the full-time housewife who had to take care of our huge, five-bedroom family home with a triple garage. There would be a huge driveway and electric gates and fences surrounding the immaculate, extensive gardens. Dad the accountant would be late for dinner as he had an important client that needed his valuable guidance, but even though he is going to be late he would call home and let mum know so that she did not worry. We would wait for Dad to come home before we ate. We would sit at the huge dining table and talk about our day. My parents would praise me for my excellent grades and encourage me in my studies. They would love their perfect son.

I wondered if it had turned out differently, if I had been lucky enough to have parents who genuinely cared, would I be such a nerd? Would I have lots and lots of friends that I would go out with at the weekend? Would I have a best friend, someone who I could speak to about everything and confide my deepest secrets? Would I have gone to university and would I have a successful career and a huge pay packet at the end of the month? Would I get married and have children?

Yet the biggest question of all was the one that had consumed me every day for the last twenty-five years. Having the perfect life I craved, would I be happy with me? With my body, my physique, my strange looks?

Feeling glum I stopped thinking about myself and my self-loathing. I instead thought about my mum who would be sitting at home right now. She only works part time, as a shop assistant, so about now she would be sitting down to dinner, a tray on her lap and a bottle of wine on the side table next to her. Since my dad died she has starting drinking at least a bottle of wine a night. On a bad night, when she can't stop crying about my dad being gone, she goes through up to two bottles in a couple of hours. Then she falls asleep in front of the television, snoring and groaning.

She looks pathetic and I am starting to despise her as much as I did my late dad. She was mentally abused by the man; her life was miserable and yet she still cannot get over the loss of the wicked man. She loved him and it was so wrong, so twistedly wrong. I just cannot believe that she actually was still grieving for him. That she had genuine, heartfelt feeling for the man that not only treated her like dirt but also made her only child's life a living hell. What kind of person puts up with that and then gives in and throws their life away when they are finally free?

I knew that I had to think of positive thoughts, like start thinking about tomorrow when Sarah arrived. So, with the sun setting, I headed back to the tent with my bucket of water and put the bottle of champagne into it before unpacking the box of sandwiches I had made at home earlier in the day. I munched down the cheese and pickle sandwiches and drank a can of coke before I retired for the evening. I wanted to be fresh and vibrant for Sarah and knew that a good night's sleep would be for the best.

Getting into the sleeping bag, the lovely, soft and warm, double sleeping bag, I began to wonder what it was going to be like to share it with Sarah. I thought about her skin and wondered if her milky white flesh would be as soft and supple as it looks. I ran my hand over the inflatable pillow beside me as if I was running my hand through her long, luscious, red locks. I groaned as I thought of her, a loud horny groan of need and desire. So, I tended to myself, and fantasised about the next day when Sarah would be pleasuring me as much as I planned to pleasure her.

The next morning, I was woken abruptly by a loud bang outside. I quickly pulled on my trousers and shoes and opened the tent. I was so pleased to see Sarah standing there. Dressed in dark blue, baggy jeans and a black, plain, fleecy jacket that was zipped right up to her neck, she had worn her hair down and it was blowing in the light breeze. The bang I heard was the champagne cork being popped. She had opened the champagne and was drinking from the bottle. I offered her a glass but she declined and carried on guzzling from the bottle.

I must admit that I was slightly turned off by her behaviour. It was not the way I would expect a lady to act and I was actually horrified when she let a large burp erupt from her open mouth. I was sure she woke up every living creature within a five-mile radius.

She finally stopped drinking and asked me if I had anything to eat. As I opened the hamper I looked at my watch, it was barely eight in the morning. She surely was eager to see me, to be with me. I was so pleased she had made the effort to get here so early, she must have set off before sunset.

I got a blanket from the tent and laid it out on the ground that still felt damp, as if the morning dew had not dried yet. Sarah sat down before I even got a chance to invite her to join me and started rummaging in the hamper. She selected a jar of salmon pâté and some crackers. I offered her a knife but she declined, instead she broke the crackers in two and started dipping them in the pâté.

Between big, unladylike mouthfuls, she told me that the pâté was really good. She asked me how much it cost and I told her. She whistled and rolled her eyes before asking me if I was made of money.

"You must be loaded," she said again. "I wish I had money to spend on such lovely food. My crappy, absolute shitty job hardly pays anything. All day is spent being nice to people that I don't know and really can't stand the sight of. I listen to their pathetic stories about how they love Scotland and always wanted to visit here. God – they have no idea how much I hate them all."

I watched her as she gobbled the whole jar of pâté along with half of the box of crackers and I was starting to find her less attractive. She had crumbs on her jacket and a big dollop of pâté hung from her bottom lip. I was glad when she finally licked it off.

"Bloody hell that was tasty," she said as she wiped her face on the arm of her fleecy jacket. Not the actions of a real lady.

Now with the pâté finished she started on the box of chocolates and it was while she was quickly devouring those that I noticed that she kept looking behind her, as if she was expecting someone to join us. At first, I did not really think too much of it and kind of dismissed her peculiar behaviour, but I really should have paid a lot more attention to her crazy behaviour.

"I love chocolates," she informed me. She spoke with a full mouth and her teeth were smeared brown. Not a pretty sight.

Finally, she stopped eating and started drinking again. She never once offered me a drink or a bite to eat and I was starting to regret inviting her to join me. I got to my feet to pick up the jars and wrappers that she had discarded. I could not believe that someone who supposedly loved the great outdoors could have such disrespect for the countryside.

As I passed her she grabbed my arm and pulled me down beside her and I sat down hard on the blanket. She giggled, her nose crinkled and there was mischief in her green eyes. She looked around again before she pulled down the zip on her jacket.

I was frozen to the spot. My eyes transfixed on what was beneath her jacket. She was stark naked and she opened her jacket wider before finally taking it off to expose her huge, milk-coloured breasts, that were covered with a smattering of brown freckles. She took one of my hands and placed it on her left breast. I allowed her to lead as she rubbed her breast briskly causing her nipple to harden.

"Give it a good squeeze," she urged me. "Go on touch my tit properly. Turn me on."

I did as she said and hoped I wasn't squeezing too hard. It felt so good to be touching another human being and to know they liked me doing it.

Before I had a chance to take in what was going on, she pulled my head towards her right breast and allowed me to suckle her other nipple. I was fully aroused by now and did not need any further encouragement.

I couldn't believe it; I felt as if I was ready to go further. I let go of her left breast and unbuttoned and unzipped her jeans, which was quite a job, as the jeans she wore were definitely too small for her curvaceous hips and buttocks.

I put my hand down the front of her trousers and into her pants. It was the first time I had ever touched a woman in her intimate places and she felt warm and sticky.

"Do you like that?" she whispered in my ear. "I have more to show you."

She opened her legs slightly and let me push a couple of fingers inside her. She was wet and ready for me. She was just as horny and I wondered when it would be my turn for her to thrust her hands down my pants and give me some hand relief.

She pulled herself away from me and stood up. I wondered what I had done wrong. Was it all over already?

Then she took off her shoes and I did not really know what to do next so I let her lead. She then pulled off her trousers and black, lacy pants and lay back down on the blanket, on her back with her knees bent, legs wide open as she beckoned me to come to her.

"Don't make me have to finish this myself," she said in a husky voice as she caressed her naked breasts.

This was the first time I had ever seen a woman completely naked and it took me a few seconds to believe this was actually happening. I was frozen to the spot.

I stared down at her naked body, down at her lady parts between her legs, the fuzz of ginger hair and the pink folds beneath that she had put on display for me.

"I want you to touch me here," she coaxed, touching herself in her most intimate places.

"Touch me here with your lips, Billy, make me come."

Finally, I got down on my knees. I took a deep breath, because after all I didn't know how long it would be before I got a chance at another breath.

I put my face between her legs. I kind of had to improvise and hoped that I was doing it right but I really had nothing to worry about.

"Put your tongue here," she said showing me with her fingers. "That's it, keep going, keep going."

It was not long before she was screaming out in sexual satisfaction, arching her back and jiggling in delight. Her huge breasts, moving up and down rapidly with every heavy breath.

As soon as she had come, she pulled on her pants and trousers and put her jacket back on. Within seconds she was dressed and putting her hiking shoes back on. She moved fast and the speed at which she got dressed made me wonder if I had just dreamt our sexual encounter.

She then picked up a bag of crisps and downed the last of the champagne before telling me that she would have to go.

"Sorry but I have been asked to work tomorrow now, so I can't stay." She opened the crisps and had a few. "I had a great time and maybe next time I can do the same for you."

She winked at me and before I could ask her to stay a bit longer, she was walking away. She left me holding the empty champagne bottle and, as I watched her walk away, I noticed that she was staggering slightly as if she were rather drunk.

I was worried about her getting down the hill safely so I ran after her, but kept out of sight. I would see her down before coming back to clear up. As I caught up with her, she hadn't gotten very far and I was able to hide behind some big rocks. I hid there for a few seconds before taking a peek to see how she was getting on.

I was stopped in my tracks as her giggly, asshole friend that I had been introduced to before, but whose name escaped me, jumped out from behind the largest rock in the ground I was hiding behind. She grabbed Sarah in a loving embrace. They kissed passionately, feeling each other up at the same time and I felt sick to my stomach at the sight.

Sarah started to giggle when they stopped kissing.

"Did you get it?" she asked her girlfriend. "Is it all on the film?" Sarah asked. She looked so excited. Her cheeks were flushed red from the champagne.

"Yeah, I got it all," her lover laughed. "All seedy, fifteen minutes."

She took a video camera from her backpack. She played back the video to Sarah.

Sarah laughed again, this time louder than before as she took my wallet from her back pocket. While I had been pleasuring her, she had been robbing me. Her girlfriend took the wallet from her and pulled out the wad of notes it contained. She kissed Sarah again, before putting the money into her jacket pocket. As if to add insult to injury, she threw my wallet onto the ground and stamped on it a couple of times with her dirty, muddy boots.

Then she took Sarah round the back of the rocks to where there was a small, green-coloured tent. A small campfire was still smouldering and I realised that they had been here all night, probably spying on me and laughing at me as I set up the perfect campsite for Sarah.

I watched them as they quickly undressed and lay on the grass. Sarah started crying out my name and her blonde bimbo giggled and pretended to be me. It was so humiliating watching her make a fool of me. She led me to believe that she had genuine feelings for me, that she found me attractive. Instead, all she wanted to do was rob me and I wondered how many other stupid guys had fallen for her charms. She was like a praying mantis, seducing her victim before devouring them. She had swallowed my broken heart with one gulp and taken my money as a trophy. I was livid at the thought of how I had been so easily abused. What a fool I had been.

I wanted to scream. I was ready to share my life with this woman, give her my love and my body. I would have divulged my most intimate secrets. I thought I had met someone that truly liked me, but to her I was a plaything.

It was then that I realised that I was still holding the empty champagne bottle. Deep in the throes of their passionate lovemaking, they were oblivious to me being there, watching them, hating them, but I soon got their attention. The sound of smashing glass brought their passionate encounter to a sudden and abrupt stop.

Before either of them had time to react, I had jumped on top of the skinny, giggling woman, pinning them both to the ground. Sarah tried to wriggle out from beneath the pile of bodies, but before she could escape I rammed the broken bottle into her throat with all my might. Dark red blood splattered everywhere covering the blonde's face in red, warm liquid.

Blondie started to scream but I stopped her quickly. With a quick jilt of the head, I snapped her scrawny neck and she fell on the ground beside Sarah, dead but with her eyes wide open. It had been a knee-jerk reaction. I had to stop her and quickly. I had no idea I had the strength to break her neck like that of a chicken. I was impressed.

Sarah was still alive and gurgling noises were coming from her throat. Blood was gushing from the wound and she tried to stem the flow by grabbing at her neck. Her hands kept slipping and made it impossible to hold on as more and more blood flooded freely. Finally, she died and the blood stopped spurting out of her neck as her heart stopped.

I stared at the two dead, naked bodies and they stared back at me with their dead, lifeless eyes. They were both covered in blood and Sarah lay there with her mouth wide open. It looked like she was trying to say something, but she would never get the chance to utter another word again.

I felt good, pleased that I had dealt with them so quickly and with so little effort. I was getting rather good at dishing out payback.

Three killings in such a short space of time. Who would have thought I had it in me?

Did this make me a serial killer? I think it did. I have now committed a series of murders but unlike your usual serial killer I have motive. William and these two had died for a reason. For the same reason. They had mistreated and abused me.

The only problem I had this time was that I had not planned the killings. I had to quickly think about how I was going to dispose of the bodies. I contemplated burying them but I knew it would take hours to dig a hole big and deep enough to bury their bodies and all their camping equipment.

I then thought about moving them into their tent, zipping it up, padlocking it and making it look like they were away for a hike and would be returning later in the day. It would take probably three or four days before anyone became suspicious and would look in the tent. Then again, the flies that the bodies would attract would probably soon attract attention from passing hikers so that idea would not work. So, I decided on the only other option. I had a barbeque.

I dragged both bodies into the tent before picking up their discarded clothes which I also threw in the tent. I then picked up all the other items that lay around their campsite. What a mess they had left lying about. They had been a right pair of litterbugs.

With most of the evidence cleared away, I zipped up the tent and turned my attention to the ground where I had slain the ladies. There was blood everywhere so I ran back to my tent and got the bucket of water that had cooled the champagne. I ran back as quickly as I could, taking care not to spill any of the water. Slightly out of breath I reached the camp and threw the contents of the bucket onto the bloody ground. It spread it out a bit but I knew it would take a lot more water to clear away so much blood, so back and forth I went to the burn, filling my bucket and emptying it on the ground.

Finally, the grass was no longer red and had returned to a green colour but the ground was quite marshy and muddy and I trampled in the mud to ensure that blood soaked through into the ground below.

It had taken nearly an hour to clear away the evidence and I finally attended to the tent again. Before I dismantled the tent, I unzipped it and located the jacket that the blonde had worn. I got my money she had stolen and put it back into my muddy wallet that I had picked up earlier.

I zipped up the tent again and dismantled it with the women and all their belongings inside. I took a good handful of the tent and wrapped it around both hands to ensure I had a good grip, and then I started to drag it back to my camp. Every few feet I stopped and sorted the ground that I had flattened so that there wasn't a trail of squashed grass that would lead a noisy hiker in my direction.

Once back at my camp I packed rocks around the tent, in a circle. I knew this would keep the flames under control and stop the fire from spreading to the surrounded countryside. Then I got my lighter. I always carry one, just in case it was too windy for matches. I dragged the tent to the back of the rocks and waited for the sun to go down. It was a very long wait. So, I washed my bloodstained shirt and trousers in the stream, along with my face and hands that were also smeared with blood.

I dressed in clean clothes and got my binoculars. I headed up the side of the hill that was directly above by tent. I walked far enough up so that I could get a view of the valley floor and surrounding area and using my binoculars I scoured the countryside looking for any signs of life. I was worried that someone might have seen my frenzied attack but after fifteen minutes of looking around I realised that I had gotten off with murder – again.

I returned to camp, played some cards, sang a couple of songs, listened to the radio, checked on my wet clothes and ate dinner. Finally, the sun went down and it was dark. There wasn't a house, farm, village or town for miles so I took the top off the lighter and doused the tent with the petrol it contained. It wasn't a windy night so I took the matches I carried out of my pocket and lit the tent. It caught fire instantly, burning with a whooshing noise. It wasn't long before the whole tent was on fire and the rock it was hidden behind kept the bright red, hot, wild flames hidden and the dark sky hid the black smoke that billowed up in a steady thick stream.

I sat by the fire through the whole night, thinking that this wasn't the kind of heat I had planned to be making that night. I had planned to be in my tent, in the sleeping bag, with Sarah, making mad passionate love from dust to dawn. I scowled as I thought of Sarah and spit into the fire. She repulsed me now and I decided that once her body was reduced to ashes I would never think of her again.

At around midnight I got the sleeping bag from my tent and wrapped it around my shivering body. I had distanced myself from the fire as the bright glow was beginning to hurt my eyes. It was a cold spring night and there was not a star in the sky. The ground would be frosty soon, and I hoped that the fire would die down soon but I knew that wouldn't happen as I could still make out the silhouette of Sarah's body. It was burning and the smell of the cooking flesh was not as revolting as I thought it would be. In fact, truthfully, I quite liked the smell, not that I would ever admit that to anyone as they might think I am weird.

At seven in the morning I awoke, annoyed with myself for having fallen asleep. I could see the smouldering ashes of the fire that was now nearly completely out. Where there was once a tent, two bodies and a pile of personal belongings, stood a small heap of black ash. A gust of wind blew some of them into the air, carrying them off into the wilderness of the countryside.

I got to my feet and inspected the remains. There was practically nothing left, except the remains of the camcorder and a blackened, buckled and bent, metal pot that had once been a silver colour.

I went to the burn and filled my bucket before carefully retrieving the pot and camcorder from the ashes using a stick. I dunked them into the water to cool them and they hissed as they met the cold liquid.

I emptied them out of the bucket and poured the water over the ashes. It turned them to mush and using a stick I poked through them to ensure all the evidence of the murders had been extinguished. Happy that they had, I collected the blackened rocks that I had used as a barrier and threw them all over the valley. Then I dug up some earth from an area that was far away from my campsite and placed the mud I had collected over the ashes. I wanted to hide them as much as possible as the patch of scarred ground was rather large.

Once I was satisfied that I had cleaned up the mess, I packed my tent and hamper away and headed out of the valley. As I reached the valley mouth I looked back one last time. I would never come back here, just like Ben Nevis and the surrounding area, I would never return to the Lost Valley.

I took a slow hike down the mountain. I was knackered and had slept for only an hour or so the night before. I knew I would be pale in colour and that my eyes would be surrounded by dark circles. Mum would know instantly that I had not slept so I would have to sneak in when she went out for work.

I drove home and emptied the boot of my car. The camcorder and pot were inside my rucksack and I retrieved them and put them in the rubbish bin. The bin men called today so the last of the evidence would be dumped at the local rubbish tip by the end of the day.

As I got in the house I got a whiff of how I smelt. I was stinking of the smell of burning flesh, so I quickly undressed and washed my clothes on the hottest wash that the washing machine could provide. I then had a hot shower and scrubbed my skin clean. I rubbed so hard that by the time I was finished I was as red as a cooked lobster.

Finally, I got to bed and when my head hit the pillow I was out like a light. My mum woke me around teatime to tell me that Hannah was downstairs.

CHAPTER SIX

HANNAH PUSHED ME TOO FAR

I took my time getting dressed. I needed time to compose myself. Hannah had come to see me and it could only be about one thing or rather one person – William.

Finally, I slowly made my way downstairs and joined my mum and Hannah in the lounge. My mother looked very upset. She was nearly as distressed as she was the day my dad died.

Hannah broke down into tears when I entered the room. She passed me the letters she had been sent from William, the ones I had posted in Inverness. She told me that she had not heard a thing since the last letter and that none of his friends or his father had heard from him either.

"Why doesn't he call me?" she sobbed. "I keep calling his phone but it just rings and rings. He never answers. Why is he doing this to me?"

She asked me if I knew where he had gone, if he was really in Inverness. She said that he sometimes spoke to me when we were working together. I felt like putting her right and telling her that he only spoke to me when he wanted to bully me or brag to me about his sex life.

"Please, Billy, if you have any idea as to where William is, you need to tell me. I need to find him. This letter doesn't make any sense. It is as if William didn't write it."

I just shrugged my shoulders and told her I had no idea where he could be, but she was right about one thing, William hadn't written the letter. Was this my first big mistake? I should have known William would never have sent letters.

That was when my mum got involved. She told me to help Hannah find William. Mum told me to visit Inverness with Hannah and look for William.

Of course, I had to say yes and Hannah looked instantly relieved to know that she had help and that she no longer had to bear the burden of worrying about William alone. Now she had my mum, and I watched as the two women discussed William and how wonderful he was, how proud Mr McGregor was of him and how everyone in the town liked him. She went on about his football skills and how he could have played for Rangers or Celtic and what a singing voice: according to my demented mother, William had a voice of an angel. Basically, William could do no wrong in her eyes. He was the perfect son, the son she wished she had borne.

Mum told Hannah that she was a lucky woman to have such a fine young man for a boyfriend, and Hannah told her that they were to get engaged. Mum was so pleased and opened a bottle of wine to celebrate. That was when I left the room. I could not stand to watch them toast a man who lied and fornicated and who never, ever, had any inclination to marry Hannah.

I felt hurt, heartfelt hurt, and I was fed up of being looked upon as second best. Didn't anyone want me? What made me such a worthless human being that every person I knew or had been acquainted with thought they could put me down or treat me bad, or just look at me as if I was as disgusting as something that they had just scraped off the sole of their shoe?

Did my mum not realise that it hurt, that it upset me to think that she loved another person's child more that she loved me? In fact, I basically now realise that my mum and dad never loved me. I came out wrong. I was not up to their expectations and I never will be.

It was about two in the morning when I was summoned again. Hannah and my mum were both very drunk and I was asked to drive Hannah home. Of course, I did – the diligent child, dependable and gullible, that's me.

As we drove Hannah did nothing but speak about William. She gibbered for what felt like an eternity and I was pleased when we finally pulled up outside the block of flats where William and she lived.

She asked me to come up for coffee but I declined; I was still tired from the night before. So, I made plans to pick her up in the morning.

The next day she looked terrible. She had a stinking headache and she looked rather off colour. I was worried that she might spew all over my car. She was dressed in white trainers and designer everything. She was rather overdressed, I thought. I, however, had worn my usual value-priced jeans and shirt and we kind of looked odd together like a geek and a prom queen.

We drove to Inverness in silence and when we parked the car, Hannah pulled a big pile of leaflets from her handbag. Bright yellow A5 size leaflets with a large picture of William printed in the middle. Above his image were the words 'HAVE YOU SEEN THIS MAN' printed in large, bold text. Below his picture there was smaller text informing the reader when and where William was last seen and a contact telephone number where any sightings could be reported. There was even a reward for any information that might help Hannah track William down.

I had to stop myself from grinning when I saw the leaflets. I knew where William was and I knew he was never coming home. He was gone – for good.

She handed me half the leaflets and suggested that I head down to the end of the High Street while she started this end. Of course, she wanted me to do all the walking, all the hard grafting. Good old Billy so reliable, willing to help everyone and anyone in their hour of need! So off I went and did as she asked: I visited each shop and left a pile of leaflets, if they would allow me.

Finally, I reached the shop where I had purchased the hamper and the goodies to go inside. I paused and wondered if anyone would recognise me but thought about that for a moment and remembered that I was not someone that stood out of the crowd. Nobody cared about me and I could drift in and out of any shop or pub without anyone batting an eyelid.

I went into the shop and asked to leave the leaflets. The girl behind the desk had not served me the last time I visited and allowed me to leave a few. Just as I was about to leave, Hannah entered the shop; we had finally covered one side of the street. We both went to leave again when a woman stepped in front of me. It was the elderly lady who had served me. She smiled politely and asked me if I had enjoyed the champagne. I said yes and tried to get away but she was not finished; she was obviously a nosey busybody. She started to speak to Hannah, who looked rather surprised to find out that I had purchased expensive champagne. She looked even more surprised when the shop assistant told her about the hamper and the food.

Hannah had looked at me. She had a strange expression on her face. She asked the woman when I had purchased the hamper and that was when I realised that her mind was working overtime. She smiled at the shop assistant, a strained smile and asked her when I had purchased the hamper. She made a silly joke, pretending that I never told her anything even though we were best friends.

The old woman was more than willing to tell and then Hannah found out that I had purchased the champagne and hamper on the same day as the last letter from William was sent. Hannah looked at me with eyes of distrust and she fled the shop before I could say anything.

I ran after her down the High Street and found it hard to keep up. She was quick and fit and I had to push myself and was very out of breath by the time I caught up with her. I tried to grab her by the arm but missed, but the second time I managed to get her and I held on until she stopped.

She turned towards me and slapped me in the face. I was stunned at her behaviour and let go of her as I stepped back. She started shouting at me, in the street, in front of all the shoppers. I tried to get her to quieten down but she kept shouting the same thing over and over again.

"You lying bastard. You know where he is. Take me to William. Take me to William now!"

She kept telling me to take her to William. She knew the letter had been posted the day I was in Inverness and this was no coincidence.

I tried to tell her she was wrong, that it was just a coincidence but it did not make any difference. That was when she started to threaten me. She told me that if I did not take her to William that she would go to the police.

She pulled her phone from her pocket. "I am going to phone William's dad. He needs to know that you are hiding something. He will get William's hiding place out of you."

Now that was something that I could not have happen. I did not intend to be caught. People were starting to look at us, starting to stop and stare and listen to our quarrel. That worried me and I knew I had to get her off the street so I told her I would take her to William.

The words instantly shut her up and I was glad that she had stopped whining and shouting; maybe she had been a good match for William. They were both demanding and difficult when they did not get their own way. I wondered if I had not submitted to her if she would have stamped her feet and thrown a temper tantrum like one you would expect from a spoiled, young child.

I managed to get her to come back to the car where we sat in silence for what felt like an age. I was glad that she had not started shouting again and the quiet gave me time to put a story together, one that she might believe.

Finally, she spoke. She asked me where William was and why he had not phoned her or his father. That was the day that I found lying came to me naturally. I think I get my forked tongue from my father; he was always telling whoppers. I had to think fast and come up with a story that she would believe. Then I had to make sure that she kept her mouth shut until I had a chance to deal with her.

I told her that he was lying low. That he was hiding from some bad people that were drug dealers. I said that the business deal had not gone to plan and he owed a lot of money, money that he did not have.

Hannah started to cry – again, and I was kind of fed up with her moaning and whinging.

"I knew one day he would get himself into serious trouble."

"I told him to stop dealing cocaine, but would he listen," Hannah sobbed loudly.

All her makeup was gone now and the white tissue she was clutching was now beige. I looked at her face and to be honest without her makeup, she really wasn't that good looking.

She asked me if he had been hurt. I told her that he had been roughed up a bit but he had managed to escape before he was seriously hurt, and she believed me when I told her that he had to fight three big guys so that he could escape.

She loved the fact that he had won the fight. She looked proud of him and boasted about her tough, brave, hard man. It did not seem to matter that he was involved with drug dealers and I wondered how involved she was with some of the dodgy dealing that William had gotten into in the past.

Then I did not have to wonder any more and she told me about some of the unscrupulous, illegal and crooked misdemeanours he had been involved in and the part that she had played in helping him. She had sold drugs for him, run errands and she had even fenced stolen goods. Then she told me that she had stole for William's dad, Mr McGregor, who had always treated her like a daughter.

I had no idea that William was so corrupt; if I had known this before I would have reported him to the police instead of killing him. He would have spent most of his life behind bars – where he belonged. Hannah should also be incarcerated and my mind started to race as I thought about her wicked, boastful confession. I wondered if she had sold drugs to kids. Would she have slipped that low so that she could please William, so that he would buy her a new pair of designer trainers?

My insides turned cold as I had an image of her hanging outside the gates of a school. She would look pretty, be dressed to kill in a short skirt, high heel shoes and a low-cut top that showed off her pert, perfectly formed breasts to their full potential. No young, hormone-fuelled boy would be able to resist her and she would lure them away from the view of any onlookers, where she would speak to them in a sexy voice, the one she used when she wants her own way, hypnotising them into buying her illegal wares.

She asked me where I was hiding him and I told her Corrie Fee. She looked puzzled as if she had never heard of the place, which of course she would not have.

"Where the fuck is that?" she asked me.

I was not amused at her language and when she swore again I looked away from her in disgust.

Women and girls should never use such vulgar language and I had to control my temper and stop myself from slapping her hard across the face. Up until her recent revelations I had actually found her attractive. I had actually felt sorry for her because I believed that William mistreated her and never paid her enough attention. I stupidly believed that she was another innocent victim of William's abuse. Now I knew otherwise and I felt sick at the thought of being in such a close proximity to her.

Then she told me to take her to him. She tried to order me, tried to tell me what to do. Her behaviour made me want to laugh. She was acting like a spoiled brat again and I let her rant and rave, cry and moan without saying a word. She wanted a reaction, she wanted me to give in to her demands but I am not William. I am not weak or pathetic and the type of guy that would do anything for a quiet life or a chance of a quickie. So finally, when she had calmed down again, I told her I would take her to see William – tomorrow.

She was not happy about that but I told her that I was due to see him then. I was to take him fresh supplies. Of course, she stupidly believed me, but then, why wouldn't she? I have always been the dependable, reliable, gullible fool that William had bullied and abused, and I was now beginning to wonder if she laughed when William had told her about the awful tricks he had played on me.

I told her not to tell anyone about our planned trip. I made her believe that William did not trust one of his friends, that he had found out that someone close to him had double crossed him and was working with the drug dealers. I told her not to even tell Mr McGregor as he would be in danger too if he knew where William was hiding.

I arranged to pick her up at six thirty in the morning. Then I suggested that we finish handing out the leaflets. I told her it would be best, just in case someone had followed us and was watching us, someone that was after William. She willingly agreed and we got out of the car and headed back down the High Street, this time the other side of the road. I wanted us to go back. People had seen us arguing and I wanted them to see us again, this time as we worked together handing out leaflets, looking equally concerned for the welfare of William.

When I finally drove her home, I suggested to her that she wrap up well for our planned visit to Corrie Fee. She was to wear sensible shoes and a warm jumper and coat. The forecast for the next two to three days was gales and heavy showers. I asked her how big her feet were and I was surprised to hear that she had the same size of feet as me, so I offered her a pair of my hiking boots which she accepted. I told her I would bring them in the morning and that she could change her footwear in the car.

Finally, I drove home, feeling exhausted and livid. Hannah had pushed me too far and now she would have to be dealt with just like William, Sarah and the skinny blonde bird. This time though I thought it would be best to take her further afield. I had already planned her disappearance and I visited the fish shop later in the day.

I sneaked in the back door. Everyone was out front. The shop was very busy and there was a long queue of customers waiting to be served. I searched Mr McGregor's pockets and found the spare key to William and Hannah's flat. Mr McGregor owned the flat and often checked up on the condition of the property. Even though he rarely had a bad word to say about his son, I knew he secretly despised him and was embarrassed at having brought up a son with very little morals, who had very little respect for anyone, including his own parents.

Mr McGregor had once or twice hinted to me that they had spoiled William. They had given him whatever he had wanted as a child and, now that he was an adult, he believed that everyone owed him a favour and that he should not have to ask twice for anything.

I watched Mr McGregor for a moment or two before I sneaked out of the back door. He looked happy. He was joking with an elderly man, one of his regular customers. They were discussing the shinty game against Alness that was due to be played on Saturday. They were discussing Fort William's star player and as I watched I could see no hint of sadness. He did not look worried or concerned for the welfare of his son and it made me wonder if I had done him a favour.

CHAPTER SEVEN

THE CAIRN AT CORRIE FEE

I picked up Hannah at six thirty exactly. I am never late for an appointment. Ten minutes after I had honked the horn, she finally came down the stairs looking tired and the worst for wear.

She was eating a slice of toast and carrying a mug of coffee. She had just gotten up and was wearing no makeup. Yuck – I thought when I saw her. She was not very pretty in her natural state and I decided I would not like to wake up to that sight every morning.

She got into the car and we did not even exchange a hello or a good morning. She reeked of alcohol and cigarettes and I wondered if she had been out partying all night. I looked up at the flat as I was leaving and was sure I saw someone at the living room window. It looked like one of William's friends: Tony, the tall blond guy that William was always with, who was equally as nasty and vile, who often called me names. I felt a little concerned as I saw him standing there and I was worried that she might have told him about her trip and if so, did I have enough time to deal with him too before he told someone about our planned outing?

Hannah saw me gazing up at the window and she looked worried, as if she had just been caught doing something wrong.

"He came over last night," she informed me. "We had a couple of drinks. He was asking about William but I told him I didn't know where he was."

She took a big gulp of milky coffee. "I didn't tell him because he also deals. He might be the one that got William into all the trouble."

Good I thought. She really had believed his story.

We drove for an hour or so before she finally spoke again.

"I have one serious hangover," she confessed. "We drank a bit much last night. William's mates really know how to party."

Getting her makeup bag from the handbag she had brought, she started applying moisturiser to her face and neck. It took her about ten minutes to work the creamy, white lotion into her skin and I wondered if this was just the first step of her everyday morning ritual to make herself look pretty.

She chatted about the fun she had with William's friends. The three guys and Hannah had shared two bottles of vodka and a few joints. It had been a great laugh or so she said and they had stayed up half the night listening to music. I wondered how the neighbours put up with it as I imagined the loud, banging, techno music pounding out of the huge speakers that William had bought to go with his very expensive stereo. The whole building must have been shaking.

Hannah applied a thick coating of foundation. It was so thick that I imagined that she needed a scraper to remove it. Then she applied blusher, mascara, eye pencil and finally lipstick, the glossy kind that made her lips shimmer and shine and look quite kissable.

Finally, she pulled an expensive bottle of perfume from her bag and generously sprayed it all over herself. I had to open the window as I started to cough and sneeze as the car filled up with the overpowering, fragrant smell. My coughing made Hannah laugh which annoyed me and she finally stopped spraying and put away all the cosmetics.

I decided to get rid of the grin from her face and asked her if William's friends were still at the flat. Her smile instantly vanished and, before she had time to answer, her mobile phone began to ring. She quickly answered it, avoiding my question. She turned to face the passenger window as she spoke to the person on the other end of the phone.

She giggled quietly and flirted with whoever it was she was speaking with and I guessed it was Tony the guy who I had seen earlier. She arranged to meet him that night, at the flat. She told him she would be home by early evening. Then she finally hung up.

She put her phone away in her handbag and turned to face me again. She took a deep breath, and then told me she was breaking up with William.

"It has been over a long time," she told me. "I was never going to get engaged. I don't love him but I do care about him. That's why I want to see him. I need to know he is OK and tell him face to face it is over."

She had been seeing Tony for more than a month now. The relationship had started by accident. One night William had locked her out of the flat after they had argued. No doubt they were either drunk or high on drugs. Hannah had met Tony on the stairs as she left. He saw that she had been crying and he consoled her. One thing led to another and they had made love in the back garden.

I tried not to laugh. They had not made love. They had a quick bonk in the unkempt garden, next to the bin shed. Her knickers would have been round her ankles, her skirt hitched high. Tony would have been lying on top of her, letting her get dirty and cold. The drunken, sexual encounter would not have lasted long.

Hannah told me that Tony loved her and that they were going to leave Fort William. They were going to start a new life together in London. She would get a job as a waitress and Tony would become a taxi driver.

We finally neared our destination and, as we drove down the long, winding and bumpy path that led to the car park, Hannah asked me for a favour.

"Billy, I can't do it, I can't face him." Hannah started to cry again which annoyed me again.

"Please, can you tell him it is over for me? Tell him sorry. I just can't do it."

I nearly crashed the car. She had turned chicken. This had not been part of the plan and I had to think fast. I needed to think of something to say that would change her mind.

I waited until we parked and had gotten my rucksack from the boot before asking her to come with me. She of course declined my invite. I then told her that William had been hurt. That he had been stabbed by one of the drug dealers in the arm. The wound had been quite deep and I explained that I had cleaned and dressed the wound the best I could but that the wound was now infected and William really needed to see a doctor. I told her she was the only person that could convince him to come out of hiding.

Hannah looked worried but it was a guilty worry, as she no doubt regretted telling me about the affair she was having with Tony. Of course, she instantly agreed to help me and ten minutes later we were on our way. Hannah had put on the hiking boots but had insisted on bringing her handbag.

"I had no idea how bad he was injured. You should have told me from the start."

She sounded annoyed and stopped to retie her boots again as the laces had already come undone. You would have thought she had never tied shoelaces before. A five-year-old kid could do it better.

"Stop walking so fast!" she snapped. "I'm not used to running around the woods and countryside like you are."

I thought it best to slow down, to try and keep her from moaning and groaning. I walked ahead, my camera on a leather strap around my neck. I knew I would not be able to come back so I took lots of photos and collected some leaves and flowers for my journal. Hannah walked slowly behind, listening to her iPod. She did not want to be here and kept checking her mobile phone and swore a few times because she could not get a signal.

When the iPod batteries finally ran out she put it in her jacket pocket and tried to start a conversation with me. She asked me if I had a favourite band and I told her it was Bon Jovi. She made a face of disapproval and told me that she hated rock music. Just like William, she liked rap or hardcore, techno music.

She then asked me if I had ever taken drugs. I stopped dead in my tracks when she asked me this and turned to tell her that drugs were for losers. She laughed at my response and told me I should not have such strong opinions about something I had never tried.

"You know what's wrong with you, Billy, you have never had a good time. Never partied or had fun with lots of mates. You don't know what it is like till you try it so don't be so judgemental."

Her response annoyed me and I quickly, verbally retaliated. For the first time in a long time I actually swore out loud and at someone. I knew my face said it all as I shouted at her, calling her a stupid fucker who only lived for a good time and didn't care about breaking the law or about the damage she was doing to her body.

By the look on her heavily made-up face, I think I frightened her a bit and I liked that.

Seeing as she had such a strong opinion on what was right and what was wrong, I asked her views on murder. I wanted her to tell me if it was okay to kill another human being. Of course, she said no.

She thought that if someone murdered another human being that they should be put to death for the crime. So, I asked her if she had ever killed someone. She said no, of course not. Her smugness was completely gone when I told her she should not have such a strong opinion about something if she had never tried it before.

She did not like me getting the better of her and she stomped off ahead in the huff. I laughed quietly as I watched her strop off and it felt good to have the upper hand. It was turning out to be a great day.

It took about half an hour before she finally would speak to me again. She asked for a drink and I gave her one. She then asked me if I knew how long it would be before we reached where William was hiding. I gave her my answer and then we started moving again.

"So only another half an hour and we are there. Thank Christ. My feet are killing me and I think I have got blisters on my ankles from these awful boots you made me wear."

All she did was moan and we stopped for a bite to eat in a shaded section as the wind was beginning to pick up. The gale force winds that had been predicted by the weatherman had not materialised yet, but if the weather continued to get worse, I reckoned by mid-afternoon that it would be best if I were heading back to the car. It meant that I would have to pick up the pace and I decided that I might have to change my plans regarding the disposal of Hannah's body.

As we set off again, she asked me if I thought she was a bad person for cheating on William. I told her that my opinion did not count and that it was none of my business. She was not happy with my answer and she had wanted me to tell her she was not doing anything wrong. So, she decided that she had to defend her behaviour. She told me about William's bad temper. How he had hit her when he was drunk or high. I did not say anything.

She then proceeded to tell me that she knew he was cheating on her so she did not think it had been wrong for her to do the same to him. It was then that I told her I disagreed and she did not like that at all. I told her that if the relationship with William had not been working then she should have left him.

She turned red with embarrassment and told me to mind my own business. I told her she should not have said anything if she had not wanted my opinion.

"He treats you like shit too," she reminded me. As if I needed reminding of how William had always been mean to me. "You never do anything about it. You let him off with it every time and you have the cheek to judge me about my behaviour. You not standing up to him is just as bad as me not having the bottle to break up with him before seeing someone else."

I just shook my head. God knows how William put up with her for as long as he did if she was this much fun all the time.

From that point on we hardly exchanged a word.

Half an hour later, or just around that time we reached the fence that surrounds Corrie Fee and Hannah started to ascend the steps that allowed you access. I stopped her and told her that William was hiding in the trees, close to the fence where there was a hole in the fence so that he could escape quickly if his whereabouts was revealed to the men that were looking for him.

"That makes sense," she said. "I know what some of these guys are capable of. They can be real monsters if you don't pay them on time or if they think you have stolen from them."

She believed me and followed me into the circle of trees that surrounded Corrie Fee. I took her deep into the darkness of the high, green trees that were covered in new, fresh spring buds and foliage. She tripped a couple of times on exposed branches and I had to help her up, and she became annoyed when she saw that she had dirtied her jeans.

Finally, we came to a rocky section deep in the forest where I doubted even the Forest Rangers venture. I sat down on a rock and took my backpack off before having a long, much required drink of water. Hannah walked over to the fence and looked for a hole, of course there wasn't one.

She asked me where we were and I did not answer the first time; instead I took another drink. She asked me again and I just shrugged my shoulders. She looked annoyed and slightly worried and then she asked me to take her to William.

"What the hell is going on, Billy? Is this some kind of joke? You need to take me to William now. I have had enough of this. I am tired, my feet and ankles hurt. I'm hungry and cold. I want to see William and get this over and done with. Take him to me right now!"

I laughed. I could not believe it, I actually laughed at her before telling her that William was not here. She looked worried, puzzled and surprised all at the same time.

She was visibly shocked by my words and behaviour. She asked me where he was and I told her. I told her the truth. I told her that he was six feet under, buried on Ben Nevis where he was fertilising the ground and helping keep the countryside beautiful.

She laughed and told me to stop joking.

"Billy, this isn't funny. I want to go home now." There was less aggression in her voice now. I could hear the fear creeping in.

When I did not say anything, she dropped her bag and started to run, but she was a lot slower than me and it did not take long before I caught her up.

The rocks had slowed her even more and I slipped and lost my footing as I caught up with her. I fell to my knees and worried that she might get away. I reached out with both hands and grabbed at her ankles. I caught her right ankle and held on tight before yanking her leg from beneath her. She tried to wriggle free, twisting round on one leg but then she lost her balance and fell backwards.

Unable to stop herself she landed hard on the rocks. I heard a large cracking noise as her head hit a boulder hard. At the moment of impact, she stopped moving, her body quivered a couple of times but then she was completely still.

I got up and found I was breathing hard, my left knee also ached and I found it hard to bend it. I did not have time to worry about myself and I hobbled over to where she lay. Her eyes were still open and I was beginning to find that I quite liked to know that I would be the last person my prey would see before they died. I was their last memory, me – boring, pathetic me.

Because we had history I did the decent thing and closed her eyes. I then checked for a pulse but there was not one and I was not surprised when I turned her over and saw the huge gash on the back of her head. It had been at least four inches long and the jagged rock had penetrated her skin, skull and had become embedded in her brain. Blood and mashed brain matter were running down the sides of the rock and I knew I would have to wash it away just in case someone stumbled upon the murder site.

I had to kind of pull her head free from the rock when I moved her to her final resting place. The sound wasn't very nice as the rock came free and more mashed grey matter fell out, so that meant I had more mess to clean up.

I took off her jacket and wrapped it around her head to stop the blood and brain mush getting everywhere, otherwise I would be here till the crack of dawn trying to cover my tracks. I did not have to drag her far before I reached an area that was a bit flatter.

I lay her on the ground next to a pile of stones and started building a cairn around and on top of her. I started with the bigger stones and I piled them on her body. I could hear bones crack with the weight of the rocks. The heavier ones would be squishing her insides turning them to pulp.

Soon the cairn started to take form and it was not long before she was completely hidden under the slate grey stones. It took me a long time to build the cairn and for those of you who don't know what a cairn is, it is an artificial pile of stones that are usually in a conical form.

They are usually found on mountains and some are very, very old like the Clava Cairns near Culloden. They are also burial chambers and are circular in shape. Mine, however, was not very pointy or completely circular but I thought it looked quite good, considering I have no artistic talents and, after all, this was the first one I had ever built.

I could hear the wind howling through the trees and knew that once I was back out in the open that I probably would find it hard to stay on my feet especially when I had such a sore knee.

It was starting to get colder and I shivered as I put the last stone in place. It really did look amazing. Not bad for my first attempt at making a cairn so I took a couple of photos to add to my journal.

I took a seat on the completed cairn and rolled up my trouser leg. My knee was swollen – badly swollen and probably about twice the size. It was also covered completely by a purplish-blue bruise. The skin had been broken in a couple of places but the cuts were not very deep.

I found a long, thick branch on the ground that I could use as a walking stick. Using the stick, I manoeuvred around the rocks as I looked for Hannah's handbag, which I finally found wide open with the contents scattered everywhere.

I picked up the lipstick, phone, purse and other makeup. I put her bag into my rucksack and finally headed out of the forest. The minute I emerged from the cover of the trees, I knew it was going to be a long and difficult walk back to my car.

I felt like crying as I clung to the makeshift walking stick, trying to keep my weight off my bad knee.

Tears stung my eyes and my cheeks felt ice-cold as the fierce winds battered against my face. I tried to keep going as long as I could without taking a break but the stinging pain of my leg meant I had to rest nearly every fifteen minutes.

As you know I am always well prepared for my walks and carry a small first aid kit. It wouldn't be of much use to any of my victims, but the paracetamol tablets would give me some temporary relief. So, I took three with a large slug of water and started on my way again.

Then the sky turned a nasty, threatening colour of grey and the heavens opened. Torrential rain beat down on me and I felt as if I was being punished for my sins.

As I descended a rather steep part of the path, I lost my footing and slipped about five hundred yards on my backside. Rocks, gravel and twigs dug into my rear end and I cried out in pain as I reached the bottom, my sore knee bashing against a tree trunk as I came to a sudden halt.

I thought about heading back into the trees that surrounded me and resting there for the night but I knew my mum would be worried and would probably call the police.

That kind of attention I did not require. Anyway, even if I could have stayed, the thunder and lightning would have stopped me, and I felt frightened as bright white lightning bolts flashed over my head and put my hands over my ears every time the thunder roared loudly.

Finally, I reached the car park. Of course, it was deserted and I was glad to get a seat. I took off my coat and shivered violently and continuously as I turned on the engine and turned the heat up full blast. It took about ten minutes for the car to completely heat up. It took about another fifteen minutes for me to warm up enough so that I could drive home.

I cried out in pain every time I had to change gear. The pain from my knee shot right up my leg and into my nether regions. I wished I could take more painkillers but knew I couldn't yet. It would be at least another hour before I could take any more.

The long drive home had been a killer and I felt quite faint when I finally reached Fort William.

I had just hobbled out of the car and was taking my rucksack out of the boot when Hannah's mobile phone started ringing. I fished it out of her handbag and was not surprised to see that the caller was Tony. I let the phone ring out and then turned if off. I put it back in my rucksack and decided I would dispose of her bag in the morning. Right now, I had to get changed, take some painkillers, strap up my knee and go and deal with Tony.

I got ready as quickly as I could. Thankfully my mum was asleep when I got home and she was snoring loudly as she lay flat out on the sofa. Two empty wine bottles sat on the floor beside where she lay.

When I strapped up my knee, the pain got a little better but I knew that in the morning I would probably have to visit the hospital to get an X-ray, just in case I had broken anything.

It was nearly one in the morning when I hobbled downstairs carrying a blanket and covered my mum. She would sleep there all night. It was becoming a regular occurrence. I checked I had the key to William and Hannah's apartment and I drove over to the flat but parked two streets away.

I was dressed in black from top to bottom. To tell you the truth, I was not sure how I was going to handle Tony. He was a big guy that could easily beat the crap out of me. I let myself into the flat and found Tony sleeping on the living room floor. He was out of it, totally high on drugs and I was shocked to find a syringe lying next to him. He was injecting drugs, using hard drugs and I shuddered to think if this was the kind of drugs that Hannah and William had been selling and probably to kids.

The syringe was still half full of brown, dirty looking liquid. Without a second thought I injected it into Tony's wrist, into one of the thick blue veins. I was not too sure if it would work so I waited a few hours to see if it would be enough to stop his heart.

So, while I waited I had a look around the apartment. I found a box containing dirty videos hidden under the bed along with a pair of handcuffs and a whip. The find turned my stomach and I was disgusted at the thought of the depraved, vulgar, sexual fantasies that William and Hannah had played out in the secrecy of their bedroom.

In the kitchen, I found a large quantity of marijuana hidden in a large, silver-coloured biscuit tin. I took the drugs. I planned to dispose of them in the morning. The living room was like Aladdin's Cave. William and Hannah had the best of everything including a fifty-inch television, state-of-the-art surround sound system and a huge black leather sofa. All no doubt bought with the money they made selling drugs.

When I finally checked on Tony again, his lips were blue and he was drooling out the side of his mouth. He had also wet himself and by the foul smell that was now filling the room, he had also lost control of his bowels, something that is not uncommon for someone that has just died, but the first time I had experienced it. Hopefully something I won't have to experience again.

My work here was done and I was just about to leave when I had a great idea. I put the drugs I'd found next to Tony. I knew that when the police finally visited the flat and found the dead druggy and the stash of narcotics that they would think Hannah's and William's disappearance was drug related. What an ingenious idea.

Originally, I had taken the key to the flat so that I could pack up some of William and Hannah's belongings and make it look like they had run off together but now I did not need to carry out my original plan.

So, I drove home, sore and tired but pleased. My secret was still safe and I could carry on with life as normal.

CHAPTER EIGHT

WILLIAM WAS FOUND

I woke the next day early. I drove to Belford Hospital and waited my turn in the small but busy waiting area to see a doctor. The doctor arranged for me to have an X-ray and I waited for ages before an orderly finally took me to the X-ray department.

Thankfully nothing was broken but the doctor gave me some really strong painkillers which I was thankful for. I picked up my prescription and went home. I rested the remainder of my holiday and returned to work on Monday morning.

I was still hobbling but Mr McGregor was pleased to see me and got a chair for me to sit on while I worked, which I thought was very kind of him. It was harder to gut fishes sitting down, but I didn't care, it stopped my knee from throbbing.

He asked me what I had done to my knee and I told him I had tripped and fallen down the stairs at home.

I worked all morning, alone in the back of the shop. I was happy working alone and I found not having William around that I was able to work a lot faster, even in a seated position. It also meant that I could tune the radio to a station that I wanted to listen to and hear the kind of music I like. I found a channel on the DAB radio that played rock tunes all day long. If I could have stood up, I would have rocked out to the tunes big style. Nobody to mock me, it would have been perfect. Instead though, I bobbed my head, sometimes quick and hard as I removed fish guts and heads.

I was taking my afternoon break. I was enjoying a cold can of Coke in the doorway of the front shop when two local policemen entered the shop and asked to speak to Mr McGregor in private.

I worked the front of shop with the young, black-haired girl that had recently been employed. She had a pleasant manner with the customers and I was glad she did. I tried to look helpful and customer focused as I wrapped fresh fish in white paper, but all I could think about was what was happening next door. Should I be worried?

Mr McGregor looked grim and asked me to help in the front shop and the door separating the two rooms was closed. Half an hour later I was asked to come into the back shop. Mr McGregor looked awful. He was sitting on the chair he had given me and his face was ashen white.

He looked up at me. I could tell he had been crying but he was now trying to look brave.

"William is dead," he said, his voice cracking a bit as he said it.

I tried my best to look shocked and I hoped I managed to pull it off. I spoke lots of condolences, as I tried to be genuinely sorry for the death of William.

Then one of the two policemen asked me if I knew if William had been in any kind of trouble. I still can't remember what the two policemen looked like, they were so tall and had dark hair. I was scared of them but I am sure I hid it well.

Of course, I said no and I asked what had happened to him. How he died. I was informed that his body had been found on Carn Mor Dearg, just where I left his dead, pathetic ass.

Two Norwegian backpackers found a makeshift grave that had been disturbed by foxes.

Damn! I thought. I surely had not buried him deep enough. The animals must have smelt his rotting carcass and had dug up his body in search of an easy meal.

I asked Mr McGregor if he had spoken to Hannah.

"We can't get a hold of her. The house phone and mobile phone keep ringing out. We are going to go over to the flat now to check in on her. Billy, do you mind locking up? I don't like asking, seeing you are in so much pain but I really need to speak to her. She might know what was going on, why this happened."

How could I say no. He gave me a job, tried to be there for me and I had killed his son. It was the least I could do.

I waited until the last of the shoppers had been served and then let the wee shop assistant go. She was happy for getting away early. I cashed up the till, cleaned down the front shop units, then locked up. I then hurried home and waited for Mr McGregor to call my mum to break the news that William was dead.

I had barely gotten in the front door when I heard the phone ring. My mum answered and I could hear her start to cry. William was gone. The son she always wanted was gone. Hip hip hurray! Ding dong the prick is dead.

I pretended to look upset as she told me about William. She knew I had already heard. I asked her if Mr McGregor had found Hannah. My mum cried some more and, in between sobs, she informed me that Hannah was missing and that there was a dead body in the flat. It was one of William's friends and it looked like he had taken a drug overdose.

I pretended to look shocked and asked her if William's death had been drug related. That was when my mum went berserk. She started screaming and shouting at me like a banshee. It was like she was possessed. She kept telling me that William was a good person, that he had a heart of gold and would never do anything to hurt someone especially his own mother and father.

"How dare you say that!" she shouted again and again. "He was a good boy, the best."

She was shouting so much she was spraying her spit everywhere, even on my face.

I looked at her, her hatred for me, her love for William and I so wanted to wrap my hands around her throat and throttle her to death, right there, right then.

She believed that the drugs had been planted at the flat and that William had been murdered by someone who was jealous of him, who wanted to have the perfect life he had.

She looked like she really needed a shower. The drinking was really taking a toll and her black hair was greasy and slapped against her head and face. Her breath stank too; goodness knows when she last brushed her teeth.

I tried to calm her down but then she slapped me.

I reeled back at the hard smack on my left check and brought my hand up to my face to feel the hot red spot.

"William would never ever do something so bad. You will never, ever say something bad about him. Do you understand me?"

I could not believe it. I knew I wasn't the son she wanted, but now I knew I meant nothing to her. She was so upset at the loss of William, it was like a mother grieving the loss of her only son.

She walked up to me again, her hand raised, ready to slap me again.

That made me mad and I pushed her out of the way. She banged against the wall as I rushed past and up the stairs to my bedroom. I could hear her shouting abuse to me. She kept saying that William was a wonderful person, just like my father, and that I should show some respect for the dead.

It was then that I realised just how much I meant to my parents and it dawned on me that she had not even bothered to ask me about my knee. When I came in the house I was limping badly. When she hit me I nearly fell over and even though I was trying to rush up the stairs, it was obvious I was having major problems moving.

She hadn't even noticed that I had hurt myself or more likely it was obvious why she had not asked – she just did not care. I meant nothing to her and if I went out one day and never came home ever again then she would not care. In fact, she would probably be pleased.

I lay on my bed and cried for hours. I hid my head in the pillow to stifle my cries. I didn't want her to hear, didn't want her to have the satisfaction of knowing that she and all the others had broken me.

There was not a person in the world that cared about me. I was destined to be a loner until the day I died. Sometime later I feel asleep and dreamt about William, Hannah and Sarah. I relived their deaths in my mind, over and over again like a video being played and then rewound. I relived through their final moments again and again. I enjoyed every moment. Not one of them saw it coming, not one of them realised that I was capable of such awful revenge.

When I awoke I found I was no longer upset about life.

So what if my mum and dad hated me. Dad was gone and next on my hit list was my loveless mother.

Then I would get all the inheritance money and would be able to move away from Fort William. I would travel abroad, change my name, change the way I look and take on a completely new persona.

That was what I needed. I needed to become a new me, a new person.

I needed to be more confident, lose the shyness.

I would frequent clubs and discos. I would learn new skills, maybe even take some night classes, or learn a new language to help me make friends and find a woman who was truly worthy of sharing my wealth and my life.

At around lunchtime I went downstairs when I heard my mum go out. I made myself something to eat and sat down at the kitchen table to eat my ham and mayo sandwich. My mum had left me a note.

She said sorry for hitting me and blamed it on grief. She said that she was going to the McGregor's to help them with the funeral.

I had just finished my sandwich when the doorbell rang. I answered the door, hobbling all the way and was surprised to see the two policemen that had broken the news to Mr McGregor standing there. They asked to come in and I let them in trying to look composed, as my stomach fluttered nervously as I wondered why they wanted to speak to me.

They had come to ask about Hannah. They had heard that I had offered to help her look for William.

I nodded in agreement. I knew I had to say something but I was so nervous that my mouth had dried up. They asked me about the leaflet drop in Inverness and I finally managed to tell them that it had been Hannah's idea, that she had been worried and thought passing out leaflets might help in finding William.

Then they asked me about the hamper. Obviously, they had been busy. They had already been to Inverness to follow up on the leaflet drop.

They asked me why I had bought the hamper and who it was for. I looked surprised and then lied my ass off to the police officers.

I told them it was for Hannah. That she had asked me to buy it for her. I told them about her affair with Tony and that she had confided in me. Tony and she were to go on a romantic picnic. They were in love and needed the help of a friend.

The policemen seemed to believe me and I watched as the one with huge, black-haired policemen, wrote down everything I said in the notebook. He was massive. He had to be at least six feet six inches in height and he looked muscular, like he worked out a lot.

The other of the two was just as tall, definitely older but still as strong and muscular. He was the one that watched me through the entire interview. It was as if he was observing my body language to find out if I was lying or telling the truth.

The younger policeman asked me why Hannah looked surprised when the shop assistant spoke to me about the hamper and why she had run off. He also asked why we had been arguing.

I told them that Hannah was upset that someone knew about the hamper and she was scared that someone that knew William may have suspected that I had bought it for her. I told them she was also feeling guilty for cheating on William and knew it was wrong, especially because he was missing.

As we talked and talked about Hannah I remembered that I had not disposed of her handbag. As we sat there chatting, evidence to link her disappearance to me sat directly above our heads in my bedroom.

I felt like chuckling and I started to look at the two policemen differently. I was no longer frightened of them, no longer worried about giving away something that might lead to my arrest. I was starting to see them as two gullible fools who saw me as a snivelling, weak, pathetic man, who was not capable of harming a hair on a flea never mind murder a human being. These two big, hulking men had no idea what was going on, right in front of their noses.

Finally, the policemen left.

I watched them from behind the cover of the front room, beige-tinted net curtains. They sat in the police car for a while, chatting, most likely about me. I could practically hear what they were saying.

They would be laughing, making fun of the clothes I wore, mimicking my voice and having a giggle at how easily my so-called friends manipulate and use me for their ill-gotten gains.

I watched them drive off as my mum was dropped off by Mr McGregor who accompanied her in.

He told me the funeral was on Friday. The autopsy had been completed and they had found that William had been drugged before being buried alive.

The poor man broke down as he told me. Maybe his son had been an asshole but he still loved him. No matter how much William had embarrassed his father, Mr McGregor has always and will always love him.

That kind of upset me. I had never done anything to hurt or upset my parents, until recently that is, but if I died before my mother, she would not cherish my memory.

This man loved his son, even though he knew he was an asshole.

I got Mr McGregor a whiskey; it was the least I could do. I offered my mother nothing.

From then on, I treated her with the same contempt that she has bestowed on me since the day I was born. From then on in I did not care about her at all. In fact, the day I killed her would probably be one of the greatest accomplishments of my life. I couldn't wait to end her pathetic existence.

Anyway, that is not important at this time. Mr McGregor thanked me for the drink and gave me a hug – a proper hug, the first of my life and I wanted to hold on, to keep hugging and to ask him to take me home, to allow me to be his son. He needed a replacement. Why couldn't it be me?

Mr McGregor let me go and took a seat. He told me the funeral plans. It was to be a lavish service. He had arranged for a horse and carriage to carry William's white coffin from the church to the graveyard where he would be buried beside the rest of the McGregor family. Then there would be tea, sandwiches and cake at the best hotel in town.

Then McGregor requested something of me that nearly blew me away.

"Billy, you have always been there for me. At the shop, I couldn't do without you. I don't trust any of William's friends now, so, please will you help me? Will you be one of the coffin bearers?"

"Of course, he will," my pathetic excuse of a mum answered for me.

Of course, I nodded yes. How could I let him down after he said so many nice things about me?

He wanted me to be one of the main people that would help bury his son. Seeing how much this meant to him, of course I accepted.

So, the next week I dressed in a black suit, white shirt, black tie and new, black, shiny loafers. My knee was a lot better and most of the swelling was gone and I no longer limped which was probably a good thing considering I was to help carry the coffin.

A black limousine picked Mum and me up at nine thirty in the morning. We have not spoken a word since the day that Mr McGregor visited and she never even looked at me as we got into the car.

She was dressed in a new black skirt suit that she had bought especially for the funeral. The way she was behaving: the sniffling, the grieving look of loss in her eyes, would make anyone think that it was her that had lost a son.

The church was packed and Mum and I had to sit at the front. All his friends, at least the ones that were still alive were seated in the row behind me. None of them were to be carrying the coffin. Mr McGregor didn't trust any of them since the findings at William and Hannah's flat.

Mrs McGregor was distraught and my mum held her hand through the entire service. At one point, I thought the poor woman was going to faint.

Once the vicar had given his spiel, Mr McGregor said a few words about his son. Some of the things he said were not totally true, but the words were spoken by a man who truly was grieving.

They were heartfelt words and, for the first time, really and honestly since I killed William, I felt guilty. That did not last long though; my mum saw to that.

My stupid bitch of a mother also got up and said a few words about William. She humiliated me in front of practically the whole town, expressing her love for him, her devastating loss, and I knew that I had to deal with her and soon.

After the service, the horse and carriage were followed by a procession of black limousines to the graveyard at the other side of town.

The mood was very sombre and there was not a voice to be heard as the coffin was taken from the carriage by the pallbearers. William's three cousins, his two uncles and I carried the coffin to the freshly dug grave.

I thought about William as I lowered him down. I had a flash of his face the last time, just before I pushed him into the grave I had dug for him. I wondered if he still looked the same or if the foxes had gnawed on his face and hands. Secretly I hoped they had. I so wanted him to be ugly now. Deformed from bites and decomposition.

As we left the graveyard I noticed the two policemen standing on the edge of the large group of mourners. I nearly did not recognise them as they were dressed in suits and long trench coats.

No doubt they were here to observe the mourners, observe their body language and to see if anyone was behaving strangely. Obviously, they still had no suspects for William's murder and had still not found Hannah.

As I walked back to the car, they stopped me.

They asked me about Tony, if I knew him. I told them that he often hung around the shop.

The policemen took me to one side and told me that they had been speaking to Mr McGregor. He had told them that he had seen Tony bullying me. That was true but he forgot to mention that most of the time Tony had hassled me, that William had instigated the trouble.

They asked me if he had ever hurt me or physically assaulted me. I told them that he had pushed me around a couple of times but that was about it. They thanked me for my help and left.

They did not come back to the hotel. I did not stay long at the hotel either.

I had a day off for the funeral and the weekend off too, so as soon as I could slip away, I headed home, got some food and drink together and packed them into my rucksack.

It was then that I remembered that I still had Hannah's handbag. It was matt black, long and kind of barrel shaped. It looked expensive and I knew it would be. I unzipped the bag and emptied the contents on the bed. There was the makeup and perfume of course. She had a black purse that matched the bag and I opened it up to find it full of ten pound notes.

I knew she would not need them so I took the money and added it to the money box I keep in my room.

There were also a couple of photographs that I did not look at for very long.

They were photos of her in her underwear. She was wearing a red lacy bra, matching pants and fishnet stockings. She was doing some rude things in the photographs that no lady should do and I quickly turned them over to find that she had written a message on the back of both.

They were for Tony, a little reminder of his girl for him to carry about in his wallet.

There was also a packet of chewing gum and a box of condoms, three were missing so at least she had been careful which surprised me seeing as she was obviously a complete slapper.

Then there was her mobile phone. I picked it up and considered switching it on and then thought better of it. I put the contents back into her bag and zipped it up. I had to find a place to dispose of the bag and considered my options.

I had purchased a fishing rod recently so I ditched the idea of a hike in the hills and got my angling gear out of the bottom of my wardrobe. I had purchased the latest gear from 'net to gaiters'.

So, I drove to River Lochy and hired a boat. One that didn't require rowing. I could not do that on my own, I didn't have the strength. So, I got a boat with a low power outboard, loaded it with my expensive gear and headed out into the river.

Some parts of the river are pretty shallow and for wading fishing. I, however, needed to get out in the open water. I needed to fish in the deepest part of the salmon river, where I had to dispose of my incriminating evidence.

It was a lovely clear day. Not much rain at all and half grey, half blueish skies.

Renowned for salmon fishing, the river flows south from Loch Lochy for quite a few miles before it reaches Loch Linnhe. You can see Ben Nevis and the beautiful green, luscious, flat plain of the Great Glen. The water of the river is so clean; it is a natural drinking water source and I filled a couple of empty water bottles. I loved taking the fresh waters from around my beautiful countryside home. Maybe I couldn't be in the mountains, valleys or glens, but when I wasn't there, I could at least still taste it. It would bring me back to my favourite spots in an instant.

I picked a quiet spot on the river that was kind of secluded and surrounded by trees. I baited my rod with a rubber worm as I could not face the thought of touching a real one. I do not like worms and I hate the way they wriggle and wiggle. There was not a hope in hell of me touching a live one.

Once I had cast the line – which actually took four attempts, I took a seat in the boat and got out my binoculars. I checked the surrounding area and was pleased to find I was the only fisherman on this stretch of the river.

I lay back in the boat and relaxed. It was a glorious afternoon, not one to be wasted on a funeral of an asshole or my pathetic mother.

The sun was shining, the slight breeze that was blowing was warm and the river was calm. Now and again the crystal clear, silent water would be broken by a fish coming to the surface looking for food. There would be a plopping noise as it disturbed the surface, leaving behind small round circles of rippled water.

The place reminded me of my late grandfather who died when I was very young. He was my mum's father. I loved him with all my heart because he was the only person who ever gave me any attention or showed me any real affection. He took me fishing when I was about six.

We would go every Saturday afternoon while my dad was in the pub and my mum was at the bingo.

We would sit on the riverbank with our rods.

Granddad Johnny had a real one and he made me a small one out of a stick which had a bit of string with a hook attached. We would sit and tell silly jokes and he would buy me sweeties and cola. I loved Saturdays and I spent all week thinking about the fishing trip.

Then one day he died. Just like that. He was found in his bed and had taken a stroke in his sleep. He never woke up again and I still miss him today.

I waited for half an hour before getting Hannah's bag from my rucksack. I opened it up and filled it with large stones that I had picked up before I hired the boat.

I checked again with my binoculars that nobody was watching and when I knew it was safe I dropped the bag into the water. I watched it as it quickly sank, deep into the dark water.

I was relieved that I had finally gotten rid of it.

I stayed there for a couple of hours and did not catch a single thing. I think that had a lot to do with the fact that I am not very good at baiting a worm, even a plastic one, and I must have lost about eight before I finally gave in and went home.

Mum was waiting for me and asked if she could speak to me.

I followed her into the lounge without saying a word.

The cheques had come through for the inheritance money. She gave me an unopened letter from the solicitor. Mum had already opened hers and was holding her cheque. She told me that William's cheque was being divided between us but that she had decided to use a share of the money to buy a memorial bench for the park. She was going to have two plaques added, one for my dad and one for William. She wanted me to contribute.

The old Billy would have instantly said yes, but the new Billy no longer put up with crap. So, without hesitation I declined. I outright said no.

Mum was visibly shocked. She thought I would do as she wanted, just like an obedient dog that did tricks on command.

"You, ungrateful little shit!" she shouted. "Your dad didn't need to leave you anything. I wouldn't have."

She was so angry and she told me that I had until the morning to change my mind or else I was to move out.

I did not wait until morning. I packed all the belongings I had including my computer which I had bought, into the boot.

Mum watched me and opened a bottle of vodka. She had moved on from the wine. She needed the hard stuff now. I watched her fill a whiskey glass with the liquid and she downed the contents in a couple of gulps.

Little did she know that the vodka was full of painkillers, the ones that I had gotten from the doctor at the hospital.

I carried on packing the car as she watched from the landing window as she guzzled down the vodka.

Every time I passed her on the stairs she would call me names. First, she started with 'useless' and quickly moved on to 'gormless' and 'pathetic loser'. The more she drank the worse the name calling got and by the time she had staggered downstairs and had laid on the couch, she had called me a 'bastard', a 'shithead' and a 'fucking loser'. She had some tongue on her when she was drunk.

I waited until she had fallen asleep before I put the empty bottle of painkillers beside the nearly empty vodka bottle and left. I reversed out of the driveway for the last time and headed for the bed and breakfast guest house I had called while I had been packing. It was on the edge of town and was called the Country Courtyard. The name had been chosen by the owner as the back garden which was surrounded by a high, brick wall had a door that led you out into the wilderness of the countryside. It was the perfect location for me.

After a good night's sleep, I would take a walk into that wilderness. I couldn't wait.

CHAPTER NINE

A NEW BEGINNING

The elderly couple that owned and ran the guest house welcomed me into their home. They were Mr and Mrs Ferguson. They knew I might be staying for a few weeks so they had given me one of the biggest rooms where I was able to set up my computer. There was even internet access.

They were a sweet, elderly couple. Grey, wrinkled, small but so nice I just wanted to hug them both for accepting me into their home.

The room had been painted in a delicate pink shade. The bedspread was covered in big, pink roses and the curtains matched, along with the cushions and the upholstery on the seat of the chair that I would sit on when I used my computer.

Supper had already been served or so Mrs Ferguson told me, so she brought me a cheese sandwich and a glass of milk. It was the kind of thing a good mother would do when her son missed dinner and she wanted to make sure that he had something to eat before he went to bed.

From then on, I knew I would like it here. It would be a home, not a hotel, and I am still sorry that my time there was cut short due to circumstances out of my control. I am also sorry that I did not get to thank them for their hospitality.

Anyway, the next morning I went to the shop to check on Mr McGregor. He was not there and there was a message for me to call him.

I gave his mobile phone a call and he answered within a couple of rings. He sounded upset. He asked me where I was staying and I told him. He then told me that my mum was found by a neighbour that morning. She had drunk a bottle of vodka and had taken some pills.

I listened to him, pretending to be upset.

I was waiting to hear that she was dead but nearly dropped the phone when he told me he was at the hospital and that my mum was in a coma. She had not died; the cocktail of pills and booze had been enough to kill a horse – or so I thought.

Then Mr McGregor told me that she had been sick a number of times during the night. He said it was lucky that she had not choked to death on her vomit but I could not agree that it was luck. The doctor told him that if she had not been sick that she would have been dead by the morning.

I knew then that I should have waited until the morning before leaving. I should have made sure she died. She had been totally unreliable all my life. What chance was there that I could depend on her just once?

Knowing that I would have to play the loving, doting, worried son, I rushed to the hospital and was met by a new gruesome twosome.

Two detectives greeted me at the entrance into the emergency department. They had some questions for me. They had come from Inverness. Been sent to investigate all the deaths, near deaths and missing folks.

They didn't look much older than me.

The two baby-faced detectives were dressed in jeans and black jackets. They wore shirts too and nice shoes, that I didn't think really went with the jeans, but then again what would I know? I know nothing about fashion rights and wrongs.

They were both tall, but not as tall as the two policemen that I had been questioned by on a number of occasions.

One was blond and one was dark-haired, dark brown. They introduced themselves but I can't remember their names. I really wasn't that interested in them.

Both were just under six foot, which was still a lot taller than me. Good build and both were rather handsome men. The blond one did have a scar above his right eye and I wondered how he got that.

They wanted to know about the pills, the pills that had been prescribed to me. I told them I had put them in the bathroom cabinet.

Were they questioning me because they thought my mum's overdose was connected to the recent demise of William and his buddy?

I could feel my palms and the back of my neck start to sweat. I felt as if I could pee my pants. If they were on to me, they might even try to arrest me today, or take me in for further questioning.

I knew I had to try and play it cool but at the same time try and look upset about my mum.

"So why did you need the tablets? How did you hurt yourself?" Blondie asked.

I pretended to look puzzled and asked them why they needed to know about my tablets. I had to lie about why I went to the hospital. I said I fell down at work, slipped on a fish and banged my knee.

I put a hand to my sore knee and gave it a rub, mainly for effect.

I was sure I saw the dark-haired one smirk at the comment. He found it funny.

They told me that the pills my mother had taken had been prescribed to me.

I looked shocked and tried to look upset. I bit my lip and managed to work up some fake tears. Just enough to make my eyes wet and make it look as if I was ready to break down with grief.

I hoped the policemen believed the distressed look on my face was genuine.

"I am sorry to be the one to tell you that, son," the blond detective continued. He looked concerned for me.

Yes – I had pulled it off. What a pair of suckers.

They asked me why I had left home and I told them that Mum and I had argued about her drinking.

I told them that she had hit me, which was true but I told them I could no longer handle her drunken rages and I left.

For a second I was sure I saw a glimmer of pity in both of their faces, but the look quickly vanished as their questions turned to Hannah.

One of the policemen informed me that someone who lived in the block of flats had seen my car parked nearby.

"Your number plate was reported by a neighbour."

He read out my number plate from his notebook and described my car.

"Why were you in the area? Are you friends with Hannah? Were you friends with William and Tony?"

The person said they were sure they had seen my car the day before Tony's body was found.

It was when I picked up Hannah. God, how did I get out of this one?

I told them I was visiting Hannah. I wanted to know if there was any news of William. We weren't close friends but I knew the family well and wanted to let her know I would do anything to help her.

The detectives seemed to buy it. There were no more questions and they left me to go see my mum, telling me they hoped she would be fine as they walked away.

Me, I hoped not. She had to die.

I finally got to see my mum after the doctors had carried out an examination. She was lying in the bed, her arms and legs straight out and she looked like she had been positioned like that by one of the nurses.

She was hooked up to a ventilator; she was not breathing properly by herself. I hoped she was dying and I asked the pretty, young nurse, how my mum was doing.

She told me she would get a doctor to speak to me.

Ten minutes later a junior doctor sat me down and explained to me that my mum was in a bad way.

I was pleased to hear that. He then said that she was making progress every hour and he hoped she would be off the ventilator in the next few days.

I tried to look pleased and show the doctor that I was still concerned. He squeezed my shoulder as he tried to reassure me that my mum would probably make a full recovery but that was dependent on when she regained consciousness.

I was praying that she never did or she would be able to tell everyone that she had not taken the pills.

I left the hospital feeling worried and I saw Mr McGregor buying flowers at the small gift kiosk, based just at the front doors of the hospital. They were roses, a dozen red roses and I heard him asking them to be sent to my mum's room.

I kept out of sight so that he could not see me and I followed him as he left the hospital.

He called his wife and told her he was at the fishmongers and I found that funny that he would lie to her. Why had he not told her that he was at the hospital? Was there something more than friendship between my mother and Mr McGregor?

I went back to the bedsit and spent the rest of the weekend in my room. I slept most of the daytime Sunday and found that I could not sleep at night.

I paced the room until early morning, my mind racing as I continued to fret about when my mum was going to wake up.

With her big mouth, it would not take long for her to blame me for the pills. In a blink of an eye I would be in jail for drugging my mum and then the cops would put two and two together and quickly realise that I was also responsible for the murder of William, maybe even Tony, and I would be questioned and questioned until I finally revealed what I had done to Hannah.

At six thirty Monday morning, I took a cold shower and went to work. Mr McGregor was already there. He was sitting in the seat he had given me when my knee was sore. He asked me about my mum and why I had abandoned her.

I told him I had not and that she asked me to leave, but he did not believe me. He was bitterly disappointed with my behaviour and asked me how I managed to sleep at night when I was responsible for my mum being in hospital.

"Son, don't you realise, it was your fault. You left her in that terrible state. If you had stayed, if you had been there for her, she would still be OK."

. He was a short, bald and chunky man with a terribly large beer belly. He had money and spent it on the wrong things.

As I looked at him, I really couldn't imagine him being William's real father. He just didn't seem to have the right DNA. I reckon his missus was putting it about.

Then again, I reckoned that he was doing the same with my mum. Why else would he be buying her roses? Goodness, what was wrong with the world? Was anyone faithful nowadays?

She could have died – he kept telling me. He blamed me and, no matter what I told him, he did not want to listen. I told him how she had abused me, how she made me leave, but it just didn't matter.

"I have to let you go, Billy. I can't have you working in the shop knowing that you left your mum in such a terrible state."

He couldn't look at me as he said this. He didn't have the bottle and that made me mad.

"Your mum is a wonderful woman and she deserves better. Maybe best you do stay away from her."

I know I was standing there, mouth open wide. I had been a loyal and hard worker. How could he do this to me?

He said he would forward what wages I was owed to my mother. He believed she deserved the money.

I couldn't say a thing. I just turned and marched out the shop.

I was mad with rage when I left the shop. I walked down the High Street, kicking over bins and banging my fists on shop windows.

Mum had taken away my job and had ruined my friendship with Mr McGregor.

If she had not pushed me that night, she would not be in hospital. If she had only kept her big mouth shut!

I wanted to punch someone, knock their teeth out and beat the living crap out of them, but I knew that I would get myself into trouble and lately I had experienced enough attention from the police.

I needed to calm down or else someone would report me. I was getting a lot of stares and funny looks so I decided to run as fast as I could to where I had parked my car.

So, I got into my car and drove out of town. I drove and drove until I finally found a quiet place to stop and I practically jumped out of the car before I had brought it to a stop.

I ran for a few minutes before I fell to the ground on my knees. The grass of the remote field I found myself in was marshy and muddy and cold to the touch but I did not care. My mind was on other things and I screamed and screamed at the top of my voice until my lungs could handle no more.

I finally fell on the ground, crying and exhausted. Too much had happened in the last few days and I felt as if I was about to lose it. I knew I could snap at any moment and if I did not get away from Fort William, away from Mum and away from Mr McGregor, I knew someone else would die.

I needed to get away, even for a few days, so when I finally managed to summon up the strength I needed I dragged my sorry, muddy and wet ass back to the car and headed back to the guest house.

I sneaked in and up the stairs to my room. I didn't want my hosts to see me covered in mud and with a tear-streaked face. There would be too many questions.

I took a shower, put on clean clothes and I packed my rucksack.

I then went downstairs and told the Fergusons that I would be away for a few days. I would be going hillwalking.

I never took the car. Instead I used the back gate of the guest house garden that led out into the countryside. I walked and walked, my head a blur as I tried to plan my future, recall my past and worry about the present.

My knee started to pain me and I took two painkillers but they only dulled the pain a little. Realising that I could not go on I checked my map and looked for the nearest pub, visitor centre or hostel. I was pleased to see there was a hostel only a mile south of my position.

Hobbling slightly, I reached my destination and paid for a night's accommodation.

Luckily the hostel also could provide a home-cooked meal and they kept a small bar that stocked beers and sodas. I was shown to the sleeping quarters which were communal. There were eight bunk beds and three had already been taken but the guests were out walking and would not return until night.

I ate dinner alone and drank a few cans of juice. There had been a choice of chicken casserole with carrots and chips or shepherd's pie. I had the casserole.

Then I retired to the bedroom where I lay on my bed and read a newspaper that I had found lying on a table. Lying down helped my knee and the pain subsided enough for me to drift off to sleep.

I was awoken a few hours later by the sound of laughter. Two women and a man had come into the room and apologised when they realised they had woken me.

They were in their mid-thirties and they introduced themselves as Bob and Marion Wilson and Tammy Wilson who was Bob's young sister.

They were American and they changed their footwear and had a wash before going for something to eat. They were nice enough to ask me to join them, but as I had already eaten I arranged to meet up with them later.

They seemed good people and I was so thrilled at the thought of having some company.

A couple of hours later I met up with them in the room where the meals were served. They had already eaten and had just ordered another round of beers. I never usually drink but Bob insisted that I have one, so I did.

Back home Bob sold houses, big luxury houses. He was a very pleasant man, short, a bit overweight and had long black hair that was worn slicked back and tied in a ponytail at the back of his neck.

His wife Marion was a stunner, tall and blonde, with a pretty face and big fake-looking boobs and a really nice ass. Obviously, she was with Bob for his money but she also seemed lovely and just as easy to talk to as Bob.

Tammy however was very quiet. The only time she had spoken to me was when she introduced herself. She was also short in height with cropped, brown hair. Her features were very plain and she could also have done with losing a few pounds.

They told me that they came from Houston. They were on a round trip of Scotland and had started at the borders, and had travelled up one side of the country and when they reached the top they would travel down the other side.

I asked them about Houston and they told me all about the huge, tall skyscrapers, shopping malls and sports arenas. He then really got me interested in visiting America. He told me about the best hiking locations around Houston and the way he described Galveston Island, filled me with so much excitement I felt giddy and light headed.

It was a state park, or something like that, if I remember right. It had sand dunes, coastal prairies and wetlands. He said the area was a beautiful site and one of his favourite places. He also said there were coyotes.

I loved that. I felt giddy with excitement as I imagined myself, hiking over that stunning scene. It would be at sunset. The sky would be red and gold, the landscape black and dark. In the distance, I would hear the eerie call of the coyotes and I would respond to their call at the top of my voice. I would be at one with nature and nature would be at one with me.

As Bob spoke and spoke about his home town, I realised that Houston sounded huge and I could imagine myself living there, getting lost in the hundreds of thousands of people. No one would bother me there and, from what Bob had said, it was a culturally diverse city with wondrous attractions and fantastic festivals.

After a few beers, Bob was very talkative and while Tammy was away he told us that she had just been through a very difficult divorce. Her ex-husband had been a right bastard – or so Bob had told me.

Bob and Marion had brought her to Scotland to try and help her forget about the awful man that she still loved.

I instantly felt sorry for Tammy; at the same time, I was jealous of how lucky she was to have people who cared for her. I hoped she realised just how lucky she was to have a brother and sister-in-law who worried about her and wanted to help her get better

They told me I was lucky to live in Scotland. They loved the scenery and thought the natives were the most friendly they had ever met. Of course, I had to disagree but I did not tell them this. How could I tell them that most of the people I knew were either drunks, liars, fornicators, bullies or dead?

At around nine o'clock and after two beers I thought I should phone the hospital and see how Mum was getting on.

I told the Wilsons that I was calling home to let my parents know that I was okay.

I lied to them but I did not want them to know that I was really calling the hospital. I also told the Wilsons that my parents worried about me and that they liked to know where I was staying when I went hill walking. It was lie after lie but I couldn't tell them the truth. I was too embarrassed to tell people that my family despised me.

The nurse I spoke to told me that she had been a bit poorly during the day but that she had picked up in the last hour. She was still on the respirator and in a coma and I was glad to hear that.

I returned to join the Americans and found that my head felt a bit oozy. I had no idea that alcohol could have this effect and I felt warm and fuzzy on the inside and for some strange reason I no longer felt as if I had a care in the world.

Bob told me some awful jokes, but they still made me laugh and he asked me about my job, my home and everyday life in Fort William.

I could not tell him the truth so I made it up: pretended to have the perfect life, a life just as good as his sounded.

I told him I worked as an attendant at the local swimming baths. He asked me if I had ever saved any lives and I said yes.

He asked how many and for some strange reason I said four, which is the same amount of people that I have recently murdered.

Bob looked impressed and toasted me for my bravery. I told them that I owned a small flat and that I was single – which of course was very true.

The television had been switched on by our host and the local news was on. They were talking about a find on the Lost Valley. There was a murder investigation being carried out. Human remains had been found.

I nearly fell off the stool I was sitting on. The Americans looked disgusted and shocked. They could not believe that someone could have done something so awful.

I just sat there and never said a word; I was numbed to my seat. Then the reporter said that the find had been linked to two missing women and showed pictures of Sarah and the blonde bitch.

I knew then that I was in a lot of trouble and wondered when the police would link Sarah to me.

Anyone at the visitor centre who has seen me speaking to Sarah would be able to give a description.

Soon the policemen would be visiting the guest house and I would be caught.

Feeling really quite drunk from the two beers, I said goodnight to the Wilsons. I pretended I needed to go to bed.

Before I left the table, Bob gave me a slip of paper with his address and phone number.

He told me that if I was ever in Houston that I was to look him up and he would take me out and show me the wondrous sights of his home town. I thanked them all for their hospitality and as I left the room I could hear Bob telling Marion that he thought I was a real good person. I felt so happy, I nearly wept with joy. Bob actually liked me.

Even though the alcohol was still affecting me, I found a new sensation kicking in, I was feeling brave: as if I was ready to face the world and take on every swine that wanted a piece of me.

So, while the Wilsons carried on drinking, I went to the bedroom and packed my belongings. I was upset to be leaving and would have loved to spend the entire evening with the Wilsons. We might have even gone hillwalking together the next day and I could have shown off my knowledge of the local area, including the history, wildlife and foliage that we might come across.

I waited for just over an hour and then I returned to the dining room. The Wilsons were watching television; an old movie was playing and, by the number of empty bottles on the table, they were well on their way to having a nasty hangover in the morning.

Bob asked me if I was leaving when he saw I had my coat and backpack. I told them that I had phoned my parents again and that it had been lucky that I had. My grandfather had taken ill. He had been rushed to hospital and I was to meet them there.

The Wilsons expressed their condolences and Bob got up and shook my hand. He reminded me that if I was ever in Houston I was to call him.

I thanked them for their hospitality and left feeling sad. For the first time ever I felt like I had made friends. It felt good and I really didn't want to leave.

I would have liked to get to know them better but I had things to sort out and people to deal with. I wanted answers and to be rid of my mum, then I would be able to think about myself.

I walked back to the guest house. It was pitch black when I left and I got out my torch so that I could see where I was going and what I was standing in. The moon was not very bright and the stars were hidden behind thick clouds, but luckily it was not raining.

The ground was a bit harder underfoot and I wondered if it was going to be a frosty, cold night. Not that it wasn't cold enough already.

I had to zip my jacket right up as far as it would go to keep myself warm. The alcohol has also worked its way through my system and I had to stop three times in a short period of time to relieve myself.

As I walked I planned my future and it stopped me thinking about my knee getting sore again.

I thought about my new life. I would move to America or at least go there on holiday. Then after the two weeks I would disappear, be one of the thousands of people who get lost in the system.

I would change my name. I would call myself Fletcher Daniels. It sounds kind of American and I would buy a fake passport and identification card.

As soon as I got back to the guest house, I would book a flight to New York, a three-and-a-half-week holiday with a fixed return date so as to not arouse suspicion.

New York would only be a stopping point. Once there and after a couple of weeks sightseeing, I would take an internal flight to California. That's right – I did not intend to settle in Houston. I would visit Bob and his family one day, but for now I wanted to keep a low profile and stay away from anyone who knew me.

Once in California I would try and secure a job in one of the National Parks, maybe Death Valley so that I could take a trek up to Telescope Peak.

Death Valley was the only place I really know anything about, anywhere in America.

I had always loved the name. Somehow, I felt an infinity to the area and I decided that one of my hotel stops in the area would be at Furnace Creek. Maybe if I made friends with the local natives in the area around Furnace Creek, they would recommend me for a job in the huge park.

I would love the remoteness. I would live a quiet, simple life. I would not draw attention to myself.

My knee was beginning to ache more and I was glad to see the guest house up ahead. It was very late now so I let myself in the front door and crept to my room. Before I had a chance to open the door, Mrs Ferguson appeared, dressed in a blue nightgown and pyjamas. She was surprised to see me and I had not expected to see her.

She asked me why I was back and I told her that my mum was not too well. I told her she had been rushed to hospital and I was to move back home to take care of my little brothers and sisters.

I did not like lying to Mrs Ferguson. She had been good to me and I was sorry to be leaving the guest house, as I knew if I stayed much longer that I would have come to call the place home.

She expressed her sadness at the news and asked if I needed any help, maybe a ride to the hospital. I said no thank you and I told her I would be leaving as soon as I had packed up my belongings.

Mrs Ferguson was sorry to hear that and she told me she would collect my freshly washed laundry. I thanked her for her hospitality and went into my room and packed.

After Mrs Ferguson had brought my clean clothes, I locked the room door and booted up my computer. I booked the tickets to New York. I was booked on the nine thirty flight out of Inverness to Edinburgh Airport. I would fly to Schiphol Airport in Amsterdam where I would board a flight destined for the JFK Airport in New York.

I was so excited when my flights were confirmed and I had the money to book first-class tickets but I decided on economy; I wanted to blend in with all the other travellers and tourists. I was to pick up all the tickets at Inverness Airport at the check-in desk.

I then printed out ten adhesive labels with the hotel name and address before I located my passport and bankbook and put them into my rucksack.

I had a quick look at my passport photo and could not believe how different I looked today compared to just ten years ago.

I had an old brown suitcase which I used for all my clothes and I did not bother to fold anything. I just emptied the drawers and crushed everything inside before closing it. I had kept a change of clothes aside and packed them into my rucksack.

Then I returned to my computer and dismantled it. I would dispose of it before I paid a visit to Mr McGregor. I packed the computer into the boot of my car and got the rest of my belongings from my room.

Mrs Ferguson had woken up Mr Ferguson and they said goodbye to me.

Mrs Ferguson gave me a hug and told me that if I ever wanted my room back just to give her a call. I thanked them for their wonderful hospitality and regretfully said goodbye.

I drove to Loch Eil, to the spot where I had gone fishing and I smiled when I thought about how dreadful I was at the sport. My amazing granddad had tried so hard to make me a great angler but I just never managed to catch anything.

The last time I was here I wasn't taking things out of the water; I was adding to the riverbed. Hannah's bag lay on the bottom of this river.

I promised myself that I would take up fishing in America and this time I would learn how to bait a hook and maybe even use live worms.

Taking the computer from the boot, I started with the keyboard, mouse and printer. I stood on the riverbank, my feet just centimetres from the water and lobbed them into the water. They made large, splashing sounds. I looked around to make sure that I had not been heard, that nobody was watching what I was doing.

Then I got the computer tower that housed the main components of the computer and I took it to the water's edge before unscrewing the side and opening it up. I kept looking around to make sure that nobody could see me.

I took out all the individual boards and other parts. I threw them into the water, all in different directions, scattering them as far apart as I could. Then I threw the empty metal box in and watched it sink to the bottom before I got the monitor out of the boot. Luckily it was a new model, thin and lightweight and I stamped on the screen a few times before I chucked that in with the rest of the computer.

I didn't like littering or polluting but this time I had no choice. I hoped the fishes forgave me.

I then got my journal out of the boot. I knew I would have to get rid of it. This was what linked me to all the deaths.

It proved that I had visited all the locations where the bodies had been found.

Even though Hannah had not been discovered, I had pages and pages of photographs that I had taken in Corrie Fee, not to mention the pressed flowers and other foliage.

I went into the surrounding woodland and gathered some wood and small rocks. I checked that the branches and twigs I picked were old and brittle so that they would burn quickly.

I made a small fire with the tree branches and then formed the stones around the fire, to ensure I contained it. Last thing I needed was to burn down a forest; that was definitely one way to draw attention to myself.

I made a fire and lit it with the lighter I always carry. I waited until it was burning brightly before taking a seat beside it.

As the orange and red flames danced before my eyes, I opened the journal and started ripping out the pages. Every now and then I would stop and look at the pictures and my notes.

I would smile and close my eyes as I relived the happier moments on the hills and mountains and I really regretted having to dispose of the journal. I felt like I was watching a part of my life go up in flames.

Finally, the whole book was on the fire and I waited until the fire burned out. I stamped on the last burning embers, just to ensure the fire was completely out.

I checked my watch and it was nearly four in the morning so I went back to my car, set the alarm on my watch for six a.m. and tried to get a couple of hours of sleep.

Six a.m. came around very quickly and I was awoken abruptly by the beeping of the alarm. I opened my eyes, stretched and farted before getting out of the car to relieve myself. I then got my rucksack from the boot and put it on the passenger seat next to me. Then I drove to the centre of town.

I parked my car in a large car park but at this time of the morning there was only two or three cars but I knew when I was leaving that my car would be surrounded by at least another hundred cars by eight a.m. and, if the police were already looking for me, they would find it hard to locate it.

I still had my key for the fishmongers and snuck in the back door, locked back up and sat on the floor in a darkened area and waited for Mr McGregor.

I had brought my rucksack with me and while I had collected sticks I had also picked a big, thick branch, one with lots of knots and I armed myself with it, placing it on my lap as I waited patiently for Mr McGregor to arrive.

At six thirty on the dot I heard the back door being unlocked and quickly but quietly got to my feet and tightly held the thick limb of the tree in my hands.

As Mr McGregor entered the shop I hit him. I hit him hard on the back of the head as he turned to close the door behind him. I knocked him out with one blow and once he had fallen to the ground unconscious I checked for a pulse and was pleased to see that he was still breathing. I then took his mobile phone from a pocket of his jeans and placed it on the silver-coloured, fish filleting workbench.

His hair was matted with blood but the cut was just small. However, a large bump had swelled up and, if I allowed him to live, he would have a very sore head for a few days.

I worked quickly. I locked up the back door and made up a sign for the front window. It stated that the shop would be closed today and I added it was due to family bereavement.

I knew that the staff and customers would believe this as Mr McGregor had used the same sign on the day of the funeral and on the days he could not face coming to work when William's body was found.

I somehow found the strength to drag Mr McGregor's fat lump of a body over to the freezer. I put him inside and closed the door. The freezer is huge and this is where we keep the fish.

On either side of the freezer there are shelves where white boxes are stacked. The fish shop sells all types of fish but we find that cod, haddock and mackerel are the favourites. So, the shop stocks lots more of these types compared to some of the more expensive fish and shellfish.

I turned the freezer temperature up so that it was not as cold; I did not want him to die, not yet anyway, and I knew he would be mad when the ice started melting and his precious fish were ruined.

I heard the staff arriving for work and I could hear them muttering outside. They were talking about Mr McGregor.

They were not pleased he was closed again and I heard one of them say they were worried about their wages. It wasn't their fault that the shop was closed yet again. One of them even said they thought it was time Mr McGregor got a grip. He had to stop wallowing in self-pity.

They had no idea I was in the shop or that Mr McGregor was lying unconscious in the freezer.

That made me laugh and I put a hand to my mouth, to muffle the sound.

I heard them chatting outside for about ten minutes, then they finally left.

I knew he never password protected his phone; stupid old fart hardly knew how to work the thing.

I found Mrs McGregor's mobile phone number and sent her a short, to the point text message. As I hit the send button, Mr McGregor woke up.

I could see him through the glass window on the freezer door. He was still lying face down on the floor but he was awake and trying to lift his head.

He had reached around with one arm to feel the sore spot where I hit him and I could hear him curse. Finally, he managed to pick himself up and he got to his feet. He was rather wobbly and he looked a bit dazed and disorientated.

He leaned against the shelves as he picked up some ice out of one of the boxes and pressed it into the sore bit on the back of his head. He groaned as the freezing cold ice touched the tender spot but he held it there as long as he could before he finally turned and looked towards me.

He could see me peering at him through the freezer window.

He shouted to me, telling me that he had been attacked and that he needed me to let him out of the freezer and then I was to call for the police and an ambulance.

The stupid man had no idea that it was me that had put him in the freezer. Not for one moment did he think that it had been me that had attacked him.

I thought that was rather funny and laughed again, this time I didn't stifle it. I laughed until I nearly cried.

Mr McGregor had been making his way to the door but stopped dead in his tracks. He looked puzzled and rather worried.

I carried on laughing. I loved having the upper hand and I held the stick I had hit him with up to the window.

He looked horrified and he started swearing at me.

He came right up to the door and put his face close to the window. He started shouting at me, telling me what he was going to do to me when he got out of the freezer.

I am sure he said at one point that he was going to rip off my head and crap down my throat.

I let him rant and rave for a few minutes and then he started kicking and punching the door. I took a step back and waited until he had tired himself out.

Finally, he stopped attacking the door but now he was breathing hard. He then started checking his pockets for his phone.

I smiled as I held it up to the window.

The colour drained from his face. He took a step back and swore again. He knew he was in trouble.

I told him to look at the digital display that showed the temperature of the freezer. There was one inside the freezer and one outside.

I turned the dial and reduced the temperature by three degrees. It would soon start to get very chilly in there.

Mr McGregor started to swear at me again and he told me that the staff would be arriving for work soon and they would let him out and then he would get his revenge.

That was when I broke the news that the shop was closed for the day and that the staff had already been and gone.

The look of horror on Mr McGregor's face was priceless and I wished I had my camera with me.

I then took control of the conversation. I told him that if he did not answer the questions I asked honestly, I would turn the freezer temperature down as far as it would go and then I would leave him there. He knew he would be dead by the morning.

He asked me what I wanted to know. So, I started at the beginning.

I started with my dad and their friendship.

I asked him why he had allowed my dad to abuse me and my mother, why he had never done anything about it.

Mr McGregor covered his face with his hands. He looked embarrassed and, when he finally uncovered his face and looked at me again, I could tell he felt guilty and ashamed.

He tried to tell me that he had often chastised my father for his behaviour but that he had never listened.

I asked him why he had never stopped him, never forced him to stop bullying me.

Mr McGregor tried to apologise, he kept saying sorry over and over again but his words fell on deaf ears and I turned the temperature down another two degrees.

I then asked him why he had allowed William to abuse and use me.

Mr McGregor groaned and rolled his eyes. He was finding the interrogation rather difficult.

He told me that he tried to stop William and that was why he had taken the car back, but I knew that William was given the car back by his mother less than two weeks later.

He apologised again and told me he was really sorry and tried to make me believe that he thought of me as one of his own.

He alleged that he hated seeing me being bullied and that he would do everything he could to make it up to me. All I had to do was let him out of the freezer.

His lying words made me laugh and I howled with laughter until the tears ran down my face.

Just a few minutes ago he was threatening my life. Did he really think I was that stupid?

When I stopped laughing I turned down the temperature again, this time just one degree.

How dare he insult me and I brought up the fact that he had sacked me only a couple of days ago, which I did not believe to be the act of someone who claimed he wanted to be my surrogate father.

He then called me a 'son of a bitch' and kicked the door again.

Of course, I agreed with him whole heartedly: my mum really is a bitch and a real nasty one.

He did not like me calling her names and told me to stop being so disrespectful. He asked me if I cared about her, if I was worried about her.

I told him that I was asking the questions and, if he butted in again with any more comments, I would leave him here to die.

That shut him up.

I asked him about the roses. I asked him if he was having an affair with my mum.

He said no but I did not believe him and I turned the temperature down as far as it would go.

Mr McGregor screamed to me to stop and I asked him again, this time at the top of my voice, if he was having an affair with my mum.

Finally, he nodded his head and I turned the temperature up. He deserved that. He was finally telling the truth.

He sighed with relief and I was engulfed with rage.

Mr McGregor was screwing my mum. I asked him how long it had been going on and he told me that they started seeing each other a few months ago.

My head began to swim and I thought back to the funeral, my father's funeral.

I had not really thought about it until today. I remember us sitting there, my mother had been crying – a lot.

There was a big crowd; my dad was well known in the town and to most people he was a family man, a good man. Not many people knew he was a complete bastard in the privacy of his home. Neither did they know that the person I had become had a lot to do with the life I had to endure as a child.

Anyway, in the first pew of the church there was Mum, me, Mr and Mrs McGregor and William.

Mr McGregor sat between my mum and his wife, and now as I look back I remember that he spent most of the time, not only at the church but also at the graveyard, tending to my distraught mother. I remember how annoyed Mrs McGregor was, and at one point she pulled him aside and gave him a tongue lashing.

After the funeral was over I went straight home, complaining that I had a headache, which was not true. I could not stand the thought of going back to the pub that my dad had visited every night since the day I was born.

My mum and my late father's friends would have gathered together to toast his memory and there was no way I would have been able to be part of such a hypocritical act when all I wanted to do was spit on his grave, which I actually did later that day.

Sometime in the evening Mr McGregor brought my mum home.

She was half-cut and staggering around like a drunken fool. Her small black hat had fallen forward and was covering her eyes and she had snagged her black tights on something. She was a complete mess and I was so embarrassed that I could not bear to look at her.

Mr McGregor took her up to bed and then asked me if I would run an errand. He asked me to go and get some painkillers for my mum and asked me to stop by the shop and check that it had been locked up properly as he had left the new girl in charge while he attended the funeral.

I did as he asked but I stopped off at the graveyard. My father's grave was covered in flowers. A big wreath lay in the centre of all the other flowers and there was a note attached from my mother.

It read: 'To a loving father and husband. We love and we will miss you.' She had also added kisses and I nearly spewed when I read the card. I ripped it up into tiny pieces and threw it up in the air, the wind catching it and scattering the small pieces of paper all over the graveyard.

I picked up the wreath and pulled off all the flowers in a frenzied attack. I was livid, angrier that I had ever been in my entire life. How dare my mum pretend that I cared for him?

I hated him and she knew that. I threw what was left of the wreath on the ground and stamped and jumped on it until it was broken up and totally unrecognisable.

Then I spat on grave, on his headstone and I cursed his name. I hoped he had gone to hell and would suffer the abuse I had, forever and ever and ever, only hopefully his torture and misery would be a hundred times worse.

I remember going to the fish shop next and then I went the shop to buy the painkillers. I had been gone nearly an hour and a half but as I got in the front door Mr McGregor was coming down the stairs. He was straightening his tie and he looked flustered and surprised to see me.

He told me he had stayed a while to make sure my mum was okay. I had believed him but now I know what he was really doing there. My mum and Mr McGregor had sex, just hours after my seemingly inconsolable mother buried her husband. She was nothing more than a dirty old slapper.

I shook my head as I looked at Mr McGregor.

He hung his head low as if he were ashamed.

I asked him if his wife knew about the affair and he nodded. She knew and she had given Mr McGregor an ultimatum: break it off or she was going to divorce him and leave him penniless.

I asked him if he had broken up with my mum before she went into hospital.

He told me that he had broken up with her a few weeks ago but that she took it badly and he was worried that she had tried to kill herself because of him.

Now I realised why my mother's drinking had intensified, and why she had moved on to the hard liquor. It was all Mr McGregor's fault.

I told him about why I moved out the house, about how she cared about William more than she cared about me. He did not look surprised. He knew that William was the son that my parents had always wanted.

Mr McGregor leaned against the shelves and wrapped his arms around his body. It was getting really cold in the freezer and he came back to the window and begged me to let him out.

I told him he still had some questions to answer and he kicked the door again and called me an asshole.

I just smiled back at him through the glass, smiling as I turned the temperature down again. He had betrayed me and needed to be punished.

I asked him why my parents liked William more than me. Why I was not good enough. He looked at me through the glass. He had a peculiar look on his face. He looked at me as if I were a complete fool. Then he said it: he told me, he told me why but I already knew, but I just wanted someone to admit it to me. I wanted someone to come outright and say it to my face.

I sat down on a chair and started to cry. Finally, someone had told me what I wanted to hear and, as the floods of tears rushed out of me, I felt a wave of relief engulf my entire body.

Mr McGregor was banging on the glass, telling me he was sorry.

He was sorry that he had done nothing to protect me from my father as I was growing up. He apologised for letting William bully me. He knew I had more than enough problems in life than any human being was capable of handling, yet he did nothing to help me.

He apologised for shagging my mum and for sacking me and he asked me to forgive him.

He then stupidly asked me to forgive William and the self-pity I felt turned to anger and revenge again.

I got up and went back to the door and told him everything. I told him I had killed his lowlife son. How I tricked him with his obsession with money and how I drugged him then buried him alive.

While he was still reeling from my confession, I told him how I had happily murdered his cheating girlfriend and his unfaithful friend, Tony. I told him I had rid the world of three thieving, bullying, money-hungry junkies.

Mr McGregor took a step back from the door and nearly fell over. He kept shaking his head; he couldn't believe it.

I enjoyed watching him suffer. I enjoyed getting a genuine reaction out of him and I kept watching him as he took a rage fuelled fit and started pulling the boxes of fish from the shelves.

He was screaming and crying, cursing and swearing, throwing fish everywhere. Some of the higher stacked boxes of fish fell on top of him, cutting the top of his head and knocking him on the floor.

He pounded the floor where he lay and cried like a baby. He knew that if he had maybe stood up for me, maybe protected me from William, maybe he would still be alive today.

I left him there, crying on the floor but first of all I turned the temperature right down. I had to make sure he did not survive the night. He knew my secrets which meant he could not live and I did not feel sad or guilty about killing him. He knew why my parents hated me and he did nothing about it.

As I changed into the clean clothes I had packed in the rucksack, Mr McGregor appeared again at the freezer window.

He now looked a broken man and that pleased me. He knew just how I felt.

He then tried to tell me that his wife would come looking for him if he wasn't home soon. He was only coming in today to open up and discuss some orders with the girls in the front shop. Then he was meant to be heading back home.

I picked up his mobile phone again and I retrieved the message I had sent to his loving wife of thirty-five years, the one he had been cheating on with my mother. It stated that Mr McGregor was finding it hard to deal with the loss of William. He needed some time alone and would be back in a couple of days. He would not be contactable.

I then turned my back on him as I switched his phone off.

I left his mobile phone on the worktop, in line of sight with the freezer window. I knew it would torment him that he couldn't get near it. He knew he was going to die; it was now just a matter of when his body shut down and went into hibernation mode. He would fall asleep and then finally his heart would stop. Goodbye Mr McGregor.

I had changed into black trousers, white shirt and a pair of black shoes. These were the clothes I wore to William's and my father's funerals.

I locked up the shop and sauntered down the street of shops.

I checked no one was watching me and I snuck down a back alleyway that led behind a shoe shop and threw the old clothes in one of the three bins I found there.

I checked my watch; it was now nine thirty in the morning and I still had lots to do. I had an appointment at the bank and I was about to make a huge withdrawal.

CHAPTER TEN

CONFRONTING THE TRUTH AND DEALING WITH IT

I walked into the bank, trying to look confident and hoping that my funds had not already been seized by the police.

Hopefully, they had not already found out about my connection to Sarah and I would be able to get as much of my money out of the bank today as I possibly could.

I waited until the teller I knew was free. She was a friend of my mum's and she was always really nice and helpful. I think she felt sorry for me.

I asked her for an update on my bank account and passed her my bankbook.

Lilly smiled and asked me how my mum was keeping. She was about the same age as my mum and I think they went to school together. She still looks good for her age. Obviously, she has had a good, stress-free life.

I told her that my mum was in hospital and she looked genuinely upset. I told her that she had tried to take her own life and could not cope without my father. When I told Lilly this I thought she was going to burst into tears.

Knowing that I had succeeded in pulling on her heartstrings, I went in for the kill. I tried to look really upset and told her that my mother had run up some awful debts and that she owed money to loan sharks who were demanding payment.

Lilly looked horrified but she believed every word. I told her that we might also lose the house as she was behind on the mortgage payments.

Lilly asked me if there was something she could do to help. I asked her if my inheritance cheque had cleared and luckily it had. I asked her how much money I could take out today. She told me there was no limit on my account, but she was concerned that I would want to carry so much cash around.

I made her believe that the loan sharks would only accept cash and that I needed one hundred and forty thousand pounds today. Lilly looked concerned but I managed to shed some crocodile tears and she gave me a withdrawal slip to fill in and sign. I knew she would have to get authorisation from her manager and I waited a tense, worrying ten minutes while she spoke to the manager.

She came back and smiled. I tried to smile back but I needed to know if I was getting the money. Lilly asked me how I would like the cash and I asked for it in one hundred pound notes. I thought the bigger the value of the notes, the less bulky and heavy my rucksack would be.

I thanked Lilly for her help and told her I would let my mum know that she was asking for her before I left the bank.

I headed straight for the post office next door and went in and purchased seven thousand pounds worth of American dollar travellers' cheques.

When the teller did not bat an eye at the amount of travellers' cheques I was requesting, I started to purchase bigger amounts at each stop I made.

I headed further down the street of shops and to another bank, one I never used and purchased another five thousand pounds worth of American dollars.

I did this for the rest of the morning and I visited every shop, every bank, every building society and post office where I could exchange my cash. By twelve thirty I had made nine stops and had exchanged around one hundred and twenty thousand pounds.

I visited a stationery shop and bought two packs of five, small padded envelopes before I went clothes shopping.

I bought lots of nice, modern, expensive clothes, the kind of gear that I would not normally purchase. I then spent some time getting some toiletries and hair products before I stopped at a small café and ordered a cup of tea and a spiced bun.

I selected a quiet corner and sat with my back to all the other patrons. While I ate and drank I stuck the labels on the envelope and put bundles of travellers' cheques and dollars in each. The address label not only had the hotel name and address but they included my name.

Once that was done I went to another post office and posted the bundles. The assistant was young, unhelpful and bored which pleased me. She was not the least interested in my parcels.

I paid her for the postage and left the shop. I was pleased everything was going to plan and I bought a newspaper from a stand as I looked for a public toilet.

On the front page was a picture of Sarah and her girlfriend; they were both smiling. Below the picture there were details of the find in Lost Valley and how forensic scientists were examining the crime scene. The forensic investigation would take a few days and the police were appealing for the public to come forward with information that might help the investigation.

I binned the newspaper at the first opportunity I could and carried on my search for a public toilet. I had to get changed quickly. Finally, I found one and waited until there was nobody around to go in.

I went into the ladies' toilets. It was the first time I had used them in years and I quickly closed myself off in one of the cubicles, locking the door behind me.

I stood there, for what felt like hours with my back pressed against the door. I felt as if I were about to take a panic attack or maybe even a heart attack. I was trying to keep it together and my hands shook and I found it hard to unbutton my shirt.

I finally took off my shirt and then took off the white vest I wore underneath. It was a tight-fitting vest, which pushed in my small breasts and gave the appearance that I was a man.

I took one of the white bras I had purchased from a bag and ripped off the tag. I tried to put the bra on and found it difficult to get the clips fastened so I turned it round and fastened it and then turned it back.

I then took off my shoes, socks and trousers and took out a knee length, navy blue skirt and a peach-coloured, long sleeve blouse that were both size ten. I put them on and they fitted perfectly. I then took off the boxer shorts I wore and I put on the frilly, white panties.

I tried to put on a pair of navy tights as I thought they would hide my hairy legs. I hadn't shaved in years and they were a hairy mess. I would need an industrial strength shaver to get rid of the forests of black hair that had grown freely all over my pasty white legs. So, if you imagine the mess of my legs, I don't have to go into details about my armpits.

I ripped the first two pairs of tights as I tried to pull them up my legs. I put fingers right through them as I tried to pull them up quickly and without care.

I forgot how flimsy and delicate they were, but with more care and attention and a lot of patience, I finally got them on.

I had also bought three pairs of shoes. I took out the navy pair. They were simple court shoes with a two-inch heel that I hoped would be comfortable and that I would be able to walk in them.

Dressed like a lady, I sat on the toilet and had a little cry. I had not been a female for years. Yes, I had lady parts, breasts and my monthly period, but I had hidden this true side of my life so long, I wondered if I could become a woman again.

For a long time, I had been known as Billy Hunter Donaldson, unofficially though and only people that knew me called me that name.

I picked the name Billy because it the closest I could have to calling myself William. I was trying to be the son my father craved as much as I could, in every detail. I had never managed to pull it off. I had never lived up to the wonderful William.

I had given in to my father's wish about eight years ago. I had decided to be more masculine, to be male, just as he wanted me to be or rather what he wished I had been.

I thought if I acted like a man, dressed like a man and did manly things that he might actually love me and accept me as his child.

It had been my dad's birthday and I had bought him a really nice present. I had bought him a shirt, a jumper and a new pair of slippers. As he opened his present I could see his disappointment, his dislike of the gift and he discarded it to one side before even looking at it properly.

I watched him, tears building up in my eyes as I felt hurt. He did not want my gift. I asked him what was wrong with the present and he told me that he had wanted a dartboard and some new darts. Not a girly present like the one I had bought.

I ran to my room crying. My mum just sat there and did not say a thing. She let him hurt me, she let him bully me.

After I stopped feeling sorry for myself I went into the bathroom and cut off all my hair.

My long ringlets fell into the sink and I cut my hair as short as I could. It looked odd and my hair was not even; there were short bits and long bits and I kind of looked like a freak.

Then I went to my parents' room and took one of my dad's shirts and a pair of his trousers. I put them on and looked at myself in the mirror. They were huge on me, but that did not matter because I looked like a man.

Then I went downstairs and stood in the living room, in front of my father. You should have seen the look on his face. He was livid and rather embarrassed. He asked me if I had gone mad and my mum started to cry and ran out of the room.

During all this hysteria, I remained calm and in control and I told him my name was Billy from now on and that Bunty was gone. I was now his son.

Then I calmly walked out the room. I returned to my bedroom and emptied my wardrobe and pulled down every poster I had on the wall of every rock star I had ever fancied. From then on, I liked women. I would stop shaving my legs and under my arms and started to try and speak in a deeper voice.

The next morning after I changed into Billy my mum dragged me to the hairdressers where the stylist had no option but to cut off the remaining hair.

I liked the look. It made me look even more masculine, well at least I thought so.

I left my mum outside the hairdressers. She begged me to come home but I went shopping for new clothes.

I could not understand why she was upset. While I was growing up she would dress me in nothing but trousers and shirts. I looked like a tomboy. She was just as bad as my dad; she didn't want a daughter either and she made that perfectly obvious.

That was why I was bullied at school and called names. That was why none of the other girls would play with me and from as young as eight years old I was called some horrible names that I will never forget. Children can be so cruel. It's hard growing up if you are different.

I was beaten up, had dog shit thrown at me, had my lunch money stolen just about every day and the other girls in the school would not let me use the female toilets which meant I wet myself a lot at primary school.

When I had got home the day after I had announced that I was now Billy, I changed into a pair of black combat trousers, green checked shirt and black Doc Martin type shoes.

I had bought some extremely tight vests, that squeezed my breasts flat. For the first couple of months my chest ached a bit, but I grinned and bore the pain. I was determined to become a boy.

I tried putting some socks down the front of my boxer shorts to give the effect that I had a healthy package, make girls think I was well endowed but it just looked stupid. It made me look like I had a huge growth attached to my genitals, so I gave up on that idea pretty quickly.

When I went downstairs and showed my parents my new look, my dad went nuts.

I found his reaction hypocritical; after all he had always wanted a son and now I had given him what he wanted.

We had a family holiday to Malta booked and he cancelled the trip as I now looked nothing like my passport picture.

Finally, I left the toilet cubical and gasped as I caught sight of myself in the mirror.

I looked so pale and my skin was a bit blotchy. I hadn't really taken good care of my skin since I had become Billy and seldom looked in the mirror.

I was dressed like a girl, I had breasts again, but my short, unkempt hair didn't look right at all. I needed to make some changes. I had to look more feminine.

Along with the clothes and shoes I had bought, I had spent a fortune on makeup. I forgot how expensive it was to be a woman.

I poured the content of the shopping bag containing makeup, hairbrushes and accessories onto the sink counter.

I found the liquid foundation and started to apply the light beige shade to my white face. Powder foundation was next, then some pale pink blusher. I applied this to my high cheekbones. Mascara was then applied with a shaky hand. It made me realise just how nervous I was feeling about what I had planned to do next.

I looked at my made-up face in the mirror. I was starting to look nice, or so I thought. I felt like the ugly duckling in the Hans Christian Andersen story. Billy had been ugly and unloved; maybe the new Bunty, the stronger and braver Bunty, not the old Bunty, would be beautiful and loved.

My hair still looked pretty awful and I used some hair wax to fluff up my short hair and tried to set it in a more, bouffant feminine style. I finished it off with some hairspray and then I applied some perfume. I had bought a bottle of the same scent I had worn before becoming Billy.

All done, I stood in front of the mirror again and admired my reflection. I definitely looked better as a girl.

As the toilets were empty I walked up and down the length of the room trying to get a feel for my new, high heeled shoes. I stumbled a few times but I soon got the hang of it. I suppose it is like riding a bike, once you learn you never forget.

I did not wear them very often in the past, not outside the house anyway. Back then, I was not confident enough and was scared that people I knew might laugh at me. So, I kept a few pairs of shoes under my bed with different heel heights. I would prance up and down my bedroom like a supermodel.

I emptied my rucksack of the rest of the money I had and took out any other belongings I might need like my passport and information on my hotel and flights. I then put all the manly clothes I had taken off into the bag and rammed it into the small bin I found next to the sinks.

I took a new, trendy looking navy handbag from one of the shopping bags, removed the tags and put the money, passport, holiday documents and makeup in the bag. I then picked up the shopping bags and quickly put them down again.

I had forgotten to put on the jewellery I bought and I fished it out of one of the shopping bags. I put on the necklace and the two rings and found it sore and difficult putting on the earrings. I had not worn pierced earrings for a long time and it stung a bit but I finally got them through the nearly closed holes.

Picking up my bags again, I took a deep breath and headed out into the streets as Bunty Mary Donaldson.

I went to a shop nearby and bought a holdall before hailing a cab. Getting in I instructed the driver to take me to Belford Hospital. I had to speak to my mum before I left for good.

CHAPTER ELEVEN

FAREWELL SCOTLAND

I arrived at the hospital at around three thirty in the afternoon.

Visiting time had started and I knew it was the best time to go and see my mum.

As I walked through the hospital doors I saw the two detectives that had questioned me about William, Hannah and Tony. They were stopping people and showing them a photograph.

It was a picture of me or rather a picture of Billy: a sketch that one of their artists must have drawn and it looked quite good, from a distance anyway.

I walked towards them, trying to keep calm and trying to avoid their attention but I realised they were stopping everyone. I made my way to them, walking slowly, trying to keep calm as I worried that they might still recognise me. My stiletto shoes tapped on the tiled floor with every step as my heart raced. I felt sick to my stomach.

I was finally right in front of them and the tall blond officer held the photograph to my face. It really did look like Billy but for some reason they had given the man's face a ten o'clock shadow to make it look like he was unshaven, unkempt. Thing is, I have never had a whisker on my chin.

He asked me if I had ever seen the person and I shook my head. I thought it best not to speak, as I might give myself away. They might recognise my voice, it was a chance I couldn't take.

He held it there a little while longer and then finally he told me to go on. I could tell he was pissed off. He had let Billy escape and now he didn't know where he was. He had no idea he had just let his suspect go again.

I waited until I had distanced myself from the two detectives before I took a deep breath. I was sure I had held my breath the entire time I was with the detectives and I am sure that if I had been kept there any longer that I would have probably started to turn blue.

I quickened my pace and headed for the gift shop where I bought a big box of chocolates. I then headed straight to my mum's room and was met by the nurse I had seen on a previous visit.

She smiled and asked me who I was visiting. She hadn't recognised me either.

I told her I was here to see Mrs Donaldson and that I was a friend from work. I also asked for an update on her condition as the nurse took the chocolates from me to keep safe until my mum woke up.

I was informed that my mum had been taken off the respirator but that she had not woken up yet.

She took me to her room and got me a chair before leaving us alone.

I waited a few minutes and then I leaned in and spoke to my mum. I had found my voice again. My real voice was back and it felt good to hear me speaking the way I was meant to, with the voice I had been given, not the fake one I had used for the last eight years.

"Hi Mum," I said. "Guess who it is."

It was weird hearing my voice, my vocal chords sounded a bit strained. The sound coming out my mouth was feminine and a bit high pitched. I'm sure after a few days of speaking like a woman again, my voice would sound right again.

I watched her face, expecting to see he open her eyes in shock, dread and horror but nothing happened.

"I heard you are going to be OK," I continued. That had not been my plan.

I was sure I saw her eyes move under her shut eyelids. I had got a response. I knew she could hear me.

"I am sorry I tried to kill you but you forced me to do it. You caused this, not me. It is all your fault, yours and dad's."

Mum just lay there, and I stroked her forehead and looked down at her old, sad and tired face.

"I know all about what you have been up to lately. Your poor husband barely cold in the grave and you started screwing his best friend in our home, in his bed. Don't worry though, he has been taught a lesson too."

I thought about Mr McGregor; he probably would be just about dead now. Frozen to the spot where he would be sitting, cuddling himself, trying to stay warm. I hoped icicles had formed on his face and imagined him and his clothes, covered in white frost. Nobody would find him for days. By then I would be long gone.

Getting up from my seat I fixed her bed sheets even though they were fine.

"Everything happens for a reason. I would have never done these awful things if my parents had loved me for who I am. You could have saved me from the awful life I had to endure. You are a pathetic excuse of a mother. People died because of you."

I leant right over her, into her face. "I hate you." I said it with so much venom that I actually spat the words into her face.

"You made me feel like I should never have been born. You made me hate being who I am and turned me into someone else. I am your daughter," I kept saying to her over and over again, right into her face.

I so wished she would open her eyes so she could see just how much I hated and despised her.

I let her know that it was not my fault that she could have no more kids and that she could never produce my father a son.

I was sure she could hear me, or at least I hoped she heard every word. I liked the thought that she was trapped in the coma, unable to respond, unable to move but hearing that I had wanted her dead. That she meant nothing to me. I hope it was causing her great pain. I hoped my hatred was killing her.

I bent forward again and whispered in her ear.

I let her know I was going to spare her. Let her know that she was lucky, that William, Hannah, Tony and Mr McGregor had not been.

She could live and I knew it would be worse for her than death. She would be left behind. She would have to live in Fort William, her name tainted by her evil, twisted, murderous daughter who had vanished off the face of the earth.

I took my seat again and sat there in silence for a while as I gathered my thoughts and reflected on how the last couple of months had changed my life completely and turned me into a murderer.

Life would never be the same again. I hadn't been able to change my past. It had come back and I was female again, but I had changed the future. I believed Fort William would be a better place without some of my victims, maybe without all of them.

They were all selfish, incapable of showing true love or staying faithful to anyone that cared about them. I had been there for all of them. I wanted and tried to be part of their lives and they shut me out. They abused and used me. Now they never had the chance of hurting anyone else. That thought made me feel justified in my recent actions. In fact, I felt like a modern-day vigilante who rid the world of the unrighteous so the good people of Fort William could have a better life.

I sighed heavily and then smiled. It was time to go, but first a quick check of my hair and makeup – wow I was getting back into being a woman very quickly. I took out the compact from the bag of makeup and reapplied some lipstick. I looked good. I looked female. Billy was disappearing by the second.

I stopped by the side of the bed, lingered only for a second, then walked out of the room. My life here was over. Good bye, Mum.

I walked through the hospital, my head held high, and my stiletto heels chinking on the highly polished floor. I walked right past the two detectives and they did not even notice me, so at the end of the corridor I lingered, pretending to be searching for something in my bag.

It was so funny to watch them asking people if they had seen me when I was standing right there, just metres away. I felt like walking past them again, but I reckoned I could be pushing my luck, so instead I headed for the exit.

I hailed a taxi and asked the driver if he could take me to the bus station.

Forty-five minutes later I boarded a bus to Inverness where I would get the plane to Edinburgh.

I sat near the back of the bus and managed to get a window seat even though the bus was nearly full. An elderly gentleman took the seat beside me and I smiled before returning my attention to what was going on outside.

As the bus pulled out of the station, I whispered goodbye to my hometown. I could feel tears forming in my eyes but I held them back. I didn't want to cry and make a scene.

I sat on the bus as it travelled the country roads that linked Inverness to Fort William. I stared at the green lush fields and hills, the grey, craggy mountains and the beautiful trees of the Scottish landscape. Every blink of my eye, I felt like I was taking a photograph, a snapshot that would be stored in my head instead of a camera. I walked in those fields, I ran naked in those mountains and I spent my most happy days there. I would never forget Scotland.

Even though I know I would be terribly homesick, I would never return here and at this time I was unsure if Billy would ever return again. I knew that for now I would have to be Bunty and I really enjoyed that thought. I never thought I would enjoy wearing a bra or restricting underpants again, but for now it felt right.

I loved being me again, but part of me still felt attached to Billy. I suppose that is how someone with a multiple personality disorder feels. They all exist for a reason and Billy had been a big part of my life, even if he was created to try and please others.

Anyway, I didn't need to make a solid decision right now. I would worry about my future once I had landed in America and disappeared into the millions that lived there. It could be Billy, Bunty or maybe even someone else. Someone else that I thought I would like being more.

My home would be on the other side of the world and hopefully there, in the so-called 'Land of the Free and Home of the Brave', I could be whoever I wanted to be.

At this time, all I knew was that wherever I settled, the state had to offer the same glorious scenery and stunning views as I was leaving behind.

I would roam fields of corn. I would trek through low lands and ramble through hills. I would fish their rivers and bathe in their streams. I would then scale the highest mountain peak and claim America as my own.

After all I am the walker. The outdoors is my domain and hunting ground and, you never know, I might be visiting your area sometime soon.